Wrecks, Raids and Ambuscades

Wrecks, Raids and Ambuscades

AROUND AND ABOUT LOOE, CORNWALL

Carrick White

In loving memory of
Christine Sylvia Carrick-White

Acknowledgments

I wish to thank the following people for their help.

Gabriel Morgan, James Willis and Richard Chalkley of Spiffing Covers for their help and patience in bringing this project to fruition.

Lily Williams of West Looe for the facts concerning the lost bell of the *George of Looe*.

The late Ernie Ratcliffe for his research on the *Flying Wulf* shipwreck and his widow Mrs Margaret Ratcliffe for allowing myself and Looe Museum access to his papers.

Barbara Birchwood Harper, a past curator of Looe Museum, and her late husband Neil. We coffee'ied, collaborated, and co-operated privately, for many years about many items of local history.

Mark Ratcliffe for permission to use his photographs of the *The Flying Wulf* and I only wish that the expense of printing illustrations, especially in colour had allowed more, but perhaps in another edition.

Peter and Lucia Ratcliffe of The Smugglers' Cott restaurant, East Looe, for their many kindnesses and, indeed, many fine meals.

The Looe Town Trust for permission to use a photograph of the Guildhall stained glass window of the *George of Looe*.

Carl Wilton who lives opposite the Morval ambush site, and allowed me to park my car on his property, whilst I explored it with rope and hard-hat.

And last of all, friend John, who was happy to wear a red Santa Claus hat and stand by the roadside at the putative Morval ambush site, so that I could take a photograph from below. Have a look at the illustration again -- can you see him?

Contents

"What is fiction, what is fact

In past and future both abstract?

Who can say what has really been,

In secret, forgotten, passed unseen?"

CW

INTRODUCTION

I moved to Looe, Cornwall, in 2001 and have an interest in its local history. When the Looe Museum was under the stewardship of Barbara Birchwood Harper, I became involved with the museum. During this time, I came across many intriguing historical incidents concerning this part of Cornwall and thought they would form a good basis for fictionalised versions. Why fiction? Because this allowed me to apply imagination and speculation to the historical record, create vivid tales, and to provide possible answers to the questions and mysteries therein. What happened to the Albemarle's diamonds? Why was Lord Glyn of Morval travelling to Tavistock? Why was the Danish national hero, Hartman, so keen to avoid going home to Copenhagen? So what I am attempting to write is "faction" — think Conn Iggulden and Bernard Cornwell, rather than Schama and Starkey. Thus history is rendered engaging and exciting and, it is to be hoped, will lead the curious to delve further into the true facts.

So please take it for what it is and enjoy it. I doubt that there is any ten miles of Cornish coastline, and its hinterland, that would not provide similar stories.

CW

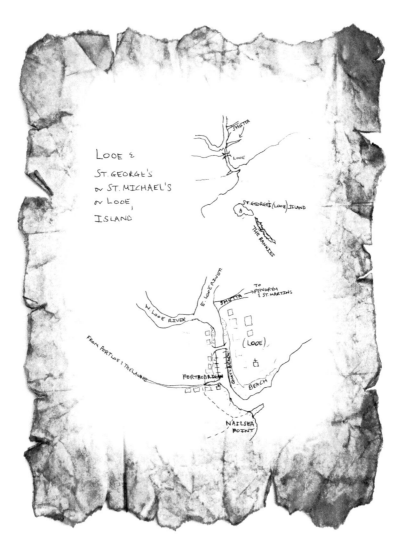

Looe and Looe Island

Peter and Pedro:
The Spanish Raid on Looe

1408

In the east, where dawn was breaking, the dazzling sun broke through the mist. And there, where there shouldn't have been, was a rock.

That was Peter's first thought, and relief followed — it was a ship. Then, alarm set in: ships either brought money or danger.

He pointed with one hand and nudged his father, Tom, in the ribs with the other.

"What, the…" his father turned. His eyes widened immediately as he took in their situation.

He swiftly turned towards their net, which was cast in the dark water, and back again. Peter could see the dilemma in his eyes — should they cut the net and leave, or take a risk and haul it in first? They faced the potential loss of a valuable net that his wife would need weeks to replace.

Before they could reach a decision, a voice called out from across the waves: "Buy —fish — money for fish." The accent was English, the language Breton. The latter was so similar to Cornish, the meaning was plain.

Tom closed his pale blue eyes for a second and sighed out loud, "Thank God!"

Followed by, "Grab a mix of what we've got and put it in that basket — lay it nice and pretty, mind." Calculation and profit-making wrinkled his brow.

Balancing in rhythm to the rocking of their small fishing boat, Peter took wide, sea-leg steps towards the small haul of fish they'd caught in their first cast.

Suddenly, their small boat was flooded with a dazzling light. Before their eyes could adapt, the unknown vessel loomed closer and the thud of grappling hooks left Peter and his father looking like the snared, open-mouthed and gasping morning catch.

Armoured bodies jumped aboard and spear points jabbed at their jerkins. Roughly, they were pushed and jostled, and forced to clamber up a hempen net. After passing through an array of painted shields, they found themselves on the deck of their enemy.

From this vantage point, as the enemy deck was much higher above the sea than their small boat, an unwelcome clarity revealed the power of their captors.

They were amidship of a large galley, whose oars were shipped. It was under light sail, provided by three masts, beneath which, sat on oar benches, was a seeming army that consisted of soldiers — spearmen, knights and crossbowmen — encased in steel and leather. Arrows were stacked in tall wicker baskets, and pikes were lashed along the bulwarks. The sails, decorated with pictures of fantastic creatures, billowed like a living stained-glass window. Between them and the dawn, another three galleys were arrayed in a "V" pattern.

The entire fierce crowd was silent. Bearded faces jutting from helmets and caps peered at them indifferently. A few breaths, followed by a single word of command from the raised castle deck to aft, initiated more prodding to drive them forward.

From ahead, his father murmured, "Any chance, jump." Although, Peter knew that Tom could not swim. He stumbled on the top step and fell flat. Hard fingers gripped his hair tightly and he was quickly hauled to his feet. Ahead of them stood some kind of foreign gentleman, who was attired in a fine steel breastplate with the rest of his large frame covered in white lace, brightly coloured silks and blood-red leather. He saw his father rapidly snatch the cap from his head, so Peter did the same.

While his father wringed his cap as if it were a goose's neck, Peter looked down towards their fishing boat. Their catch was being looted, and a soldier was about to put a torch to a small pile of pitch and timber that he had rammed under the seat where he, Peter Chubb, had sat for many an hour, in weather fair and foul. Tears filled the boy's eyes. He was drained of hope and feared losing everything that he loved.

A harsh command from the deck stopped the fire-bearing soldier. He threw the burning taper away, hissing as it hit the water. Momentarily, relief for their boat and livelihood arose, only to be dispelled the next minute at the sight of axes being tossed down, followed by heavy pounding at the bottom of the boat to hole it and the tying-off of the steering. The soldiers regained the deck of their ship. Soon, all that could be seen of their boat was a lonely, listing hull circling to its death.

The crew had no fear of them: his father's dagger was still at his belt; his own slingshot hung at his shoulder; their hands were not tied.

The grandee stared at them and the clearing mist around the ship. Then, with a sharp flick of his hand, he beckoned a bowed figure forward, who reminded Peter of the parish priest: bald head curtained with long white hair, and dark ankle-length clothes. To him, the grandee addressed a few foreign words that seemed to be instructions. The "priest" then cleared his throat and spoke in a sympathetic manner. It was the same voice that had called out to them earlier, in the Breton language.

"My master, Don Pedro el Nino, Count of Buelna, charges you to speak the truth or suffer. My Lord is not ill-disposed towards you — you are Cornish. He says that you are not of that strange and incomprehensible race of drunkards, braggarts and pirates; the English. As in truth I am. Our fates are intertwined, so speak honestly, for all of our sakes." From somewhere, a crude chart was passed to him. He laid it on the deck before Peter and Tom, weighing the corners down with objects that were also handed to him, and lastly his foot.

"Now, where are we? Point on the map."

And now a dilemma: should they betray their nearby home port, or send them off to some other poor harbour? Tom bought time by peering at the map, seemingly confused, circling and scanning the map from all directions. A rougher man, certainly a seaman, pressed forward with a compass and realigned the map. He thrust Tom to one side of it and pointed to the opposite side, and then ahead across the sea. He said some unfamiliar word and "the priest", pointing in the same direction, translated: "North — now where on the chart are we?"

Tom leaned down and indicated a point that Peter knew to be to the south-east of their current position. He then pointed aft of the ship, to the west: "Rocks, danger, reefs!" The priest translated to Don Pedro, who had been closely watching the two Cornish prisoners.

Tom pointed out over the bows to the north-east, towards Shutta their home harbour. What was he doing? Peter's mother, sisters and friends were there. His father said "Plymouth" and then swung his hand half-left to where St. Michael's Island was just appearing through the thinning mist. "Rame Head," he declared pointing to the chart again with his right hand. Now Peter understood his father's plan. Heading for the notional Plymouth, the galleys would have to sail east and straight onto the Rannies, the deadly rocky spine that stretched south from the back of St. Michael's Island.

More translations ensued. Don Pedro nodded, pursing his lips in contemplation. Further discussion and peremptory orders followed and then Peter was grabbed by the arms and pulled forward. He found himself staring straight into eyes as black as a shark's. Don Pedro, his lip curled in disdain, stared at him.

The priest's voice broke through the stare: "Is this all true?"

"Yes!" Peter nodded madly, open-mouthed, his jaw rattling. "Look at your chart, see the tower on Rame Head. There it is!" he shouted pointing at the chapel on top of St. Michael's

Island, that was just beginning to be touched by the sunlight above the disappearing mist.

"Don Pedro is not sure that he can trust either of you."

Tom protested and pleaded but hands from behind snatched his dagger. He was dragged to the side and forced to stand on the bulwark. A noose, dropped from above, was placed around his neck. He balanced there, swaying with only his sea-legs saving him from suspension and strangulation. Concentration and fear passed over his face, yet he still managed to say "Froggie!" whilst staring at Peter. Horrified, his son knew he was referring to the difference between them — a source of ribbing and humour — that he could swim and Tom could not — "Never seen the need…"

The ship was already moving east, followed by the three others. The tide was half-flood and the mist was clearing. The Spaniards were obviously discussing him. He was of no use to them, and would be next. He drew his knife and darted towards his father. Casually flourished sword points drove him back. This deadly game was an amusement for the crew; it was a question of survival and providing a distraction for him. Don Pedro was pulling his beard and, for a moment, an eyebrow rose in admiration, yet he turned away. Clearly, he had no intention of intervening either way. Tom jumped and ran and twisted. He grabbed a rope and leapt onto the ship's side and ran across the moving oars as some of the crew chased him and others made blows — serious or mock — as he passed. Others just pointed and laughed. Crossbowmen pretended to take aim, but they weren't going to waste a bolt on him.

He danced and ran; he had no other choice. His one objective was to get to his father before…

The ship struck throwing everything — live or inanimate — forward. Tom sprawled amongst a tumbling stream of men, metal and wood. Like an instantly felled wood, long oars and the masts crashed around him. The hull swung about and tilted. Peter used this opportunity to swing from something and fall onto the rocks of the Rannies.

His father had not been hung. Instead he'd been crushed between the hull and the rocks. The sight left no doubt in Peter's mind that he was dead.

He was not alone though. Many other men had been cast onto the reef. Some were wounded, others shocked or unhurt. They would be out to seek revenge. He climbed and clambered and swam across the half-submerged crags, moving inland towards where he knew he would find the island. A seal brushed him aside. The barnacles scraped and scoured him, and the seaweed curled around his legs and tripped him.

It was a long time before he climbed up onto the thick shiny mattress-like grass of St. Michael's Island, cut, bloody, and in rags. For a few moments, he lay gasping for breath, his heartbeat racing in his chest and his pulse beating in his ears.

He had expected a chase. Looking back, he could see that the Spaniards were more concerned with their own survival. To his surprise, a small boat with their leaders — conspicuous in their bright attire — had launched from the doomed ship. Its three companion galleys were standing-off and rescuing the survivors.

They were as industrious as any enemy wrecked on a foreign shore. Soon all of the wrecked were aboard; the badly wounded left to the tide. He could hear their screams and anger in the distance. Weapons and barrels were rescued from the waves and then the remaining three galleys sailed south. Perhaps they were leaving?

Broken bodies bobbed in the waves and already his mind was distractedly calculating where in the bay the currents and tides would deposit his father's body.

By the time he'd climbed the bald pate of the island to the small chapel on the brow, the galleys were far out and turning east, flanking the Rannies. Perhaps they would not see the town. From the sea, quite deliberately, little was visible as the river turned at the estuary. The port was concealed by an outcrop of rocks on the seaward side. Only a thin strip of beach and the odd hut could be seen. Surely that would not tempt the raiders?

To his dismay, he saw the galleys turn towards the land. By a stroke of ill-fortune, it was at that moment that a merchant ship was leaving the river. It had been seen.

Peter knew the danger was just about to begin. Now he was in a true race to get to the mainland and warn the town. He ran to the tiny church perched on the top of the bare island and pushed his way past a few pilgrims. It took him a few minutes, and with much relief, he found the two monks who lived on the island; he had feared that they were at sea in their small coracles. They were grubbing vegetables in a small lynchet on the landward side of the island and were not impressed by his story. He looked half-crazed. It took him another few minutes and an infuriatingly slow walk with them to the top of the island to show them the distant galleys, that were now beginning to turn towards Shutta.

At last, convinced of the imminent danger, they showed a surprising turn of barefoot speed back to the small beach and their coracles. One ferried him, the small craft, waddling across the waves, back to the mainland. The other ran to the chapel to rescue their few precious possessions.

They landed opposite the island. It was the shortest route, as manoeuvring a coracle with two people in it was difficult. Peter was away before the monk had set a foot ashore. Up the rough scree of shale, he scrambled. Ahead lay almost a mile of steep downs before he would reach the town. He struggled through the yellow gorse, its sweet smell in his nostrils, whilst it pricked his arms and tripped his feet. As he breasted the hill, cattle mooed and sheep bleated as he burst through them. Further along, dogs barked as he passed a few fieldworkers and shepherds. He was too breathless to explain, apart from pointing towards the sea. In the shelter of the down, he passed through orchards where pigs snorted and chickens squawked.

He paused and bent over, crippled by a stitch — well named he thought — as his sides felt as though they were stitched to his belly. As it eased, his thoughts raced.

There had been small piratical raids on Shutta before: single ships sneaking in during the night to steal boats and nets, and whatever else they could grab. There had been larger incursions from men of the French ports. But these had occurred elsewhere and because of the many English and Cornish ports, both big and small, people fatalistically relied on safety in numbers and hoped, that their homeport would be spared. However, everyone had been taught, from childhood, that the first task in the event of any invasion was to get the bells ringing in alarm immediately. In the past, doing this quickly had sometimes deterred raiders. He hurried onwards, considering who he should tell and what he should say — after all, he and his father had led the galleys to Shutta, however unwillingly.

Below him was the Looe River, curving in from the sea past the far sandy beach. From there it formed a long-tailed "Y", separating into two rivers just beyond the wooden bridge.

He had taken a short cut and had now reached the easier going narrow track that led around Nailzea Point to the small valley, where the harbour of Portbodriggan was tucked away on the west side of the Looe River. This was his home. Here was the church tower of St. Nicholas, the quay, the many slipways, and the fish cellars with their dwellings overhead. Further inland were cottages and houses.

He told his story to the priest, ending with, "My father, Tom Chubb, told them nothing. They were about to hang him when we hit the Rannies. That's when they spotted the ship leaving port."

Father Fiddick bossed and ordered various folk to act as messengers, to inform the Portreeve, and spread the word to the ordinary townsfolk. He tasked others with going by boat, or by horse, across to the opposite shore to warn the folk there, and to organise a defence. He also instructed them to call in reinforcements from neighbouring manors. The bell was rung in the alarm tocsin and carried from church to church to warn the rich folk at Shutta, who lived just beyond the bridge. The even richer ones were at Pendrym, a hidden valley to the north-east. At the first tolling of the alarm, they could hide their wealth or carry riches, wives and daughters further inland to the manors of neighbours. The poor fishermen who lived in hovels on the beach, and craftsmen of the cottages and crofts in the dunes behind them, would have to shift for themselves. The sea was a pathway for marauders and no person of standing would live within sight of it. Raiders came and went and had no time for exploration of the hinterland. The ebbing tide was the town's best defence as it laid a time-limit on depredations, if the invaders were not to be stranded and trapped.

Peter knew that the incoming tide was at mid-flood; considerable time had been wasted.

Looking back towards the estuary, his stomach churned with fear as he realised how close the three galleys were to the mouth of the river. Dark oar-legged monsters, silhouetted by the morning sun, bearing death and destruction, leaving nothing for the survivors but funerals and weeping and years of poverty and hunger. Despite their proximity, they were being swept in on the flood tide, making it harder for them to steer as they would be moving at the same speed as the water — in effect, drifting. That would delay them awhile.

When he arrived home, at the tiny cottage halfway up the small valley leading out of Portbodriggan, he found his mother, a baby swaddled to her back, and his three sisters. They were busy loading the wicker panniers that straddled their donkey's back with every portable item of value they had, punctuated by his mother's "Pack that! Leave that…"

She took one look at him and then dragged him aside. "Where is he?"

"He's dead — the Spaniards, galleys…" He burst into tears without realising it.

She hugged him for a moment and then shook him hard. "How long? How close? How much time have we got?"

"They're in the river!" She handed out knives and small cleavers and axes. "Right, that's it, girls. Go! Up the hill, quickly, head for…" She thought for a moment. "… Trelawne!

If we get separated, meet at the crossroads there. Failing that, Plint Church. Now go!" As they hurried away, the wail of the eldest sounded through the din of their fleeing neighbours: "Father, where's Father?"

"He's meeting us where I said, my love."

"I need my longbow," Peter said.

"You're coming with us, lad. Now! We need you! In bad times, the Spaniards won't be the only thieves."

"No! You didn't see what they did." Fear had turned to anger: the image of his father crushed by the shipwreck would haunt his mind forever — the remnants of his childhood were over. Anger surged in him again. Not the hot anger of boyhood fights, but the cold anger of a killer who would risk all and kill by calculation, without a conscience. "I can't go. They killed Father. Was all that practice at the butts on Sundays for nothing, mother?" He quickly placed a finger on her lips, then continued: "Stick with our neighbours and you'll be safe. Go!" To save further argument, Peter dashed into their home.

Here was his most prized possession, given to him by an uncle who had been an archer at the Battle of Auray, forty years before. In hard times his mother had often suggested that they sell it and replace it with a cheaper one — thank God he had created such a fuss — she had given in and let him keep it. He pulled his bow and arrows from under his sheepskin bed and took a bag from behind the door. He knew it held a fish-gutting knife. He placed one end of the longbow on the ground, then bent and strung it. He then fitted a leather arm-protector to his left forearm, tying the laces with his fingers and teeth. The bag and quivers he hung around his neck. Their cat slept on regardless, in the rushes on the floor.

Outside, his mother was nowhere to be seen; she had gone. He quenched his raging thirst by drinking rainwater from the water butt. Leaving the door open, he took one last look at his home from the road and then hurried down towards the quay. Instantly, he back-tracked. He was shocked by the sight of the bow of a galley nosing into the small harbour, its upraised oars and mast dwarfing the low buildings.

They had taken prizes already: two Cornish ships with their valuable cargoes were moving down the river and out to sea. He knew this was an incalculable loss to the local livelihoods as every village for miles invested in the building of ships and their trading voyages. So gone was a sliver of hope for better things; their lifeline from starvation during bad winters and old age. Not that his father need worry about old age.

He ran along a track that took him uphill, parallel to the river. In his blind panic, he caught his foot in the longbow and nearly went sprawling. Where were the other men? He stopped and looked over the rooftops. He could see that many fishing boats were already burning or sunken, the top of their masts pointing at different angles. This raid was for punishment, as well as profit.

Just beyond, he could see the other two galleys: one was moored tight to the bridge mid-river, landing men over its stern onto the bridge. The other vessel was anchored nearby, on a longer rope closer to the far bank. It was landing men via a gangplank directly onto the sandy beach opposite.

There was some resistance from his fellow townsmen — the odd slingshot hit the Spaniards armour or helmets, and he saw a soldier knocked off the gangplank and into the flowing river. A few arrows were fired at the galley. In response, the crossbowmen drove large wicker shields into the sand as a screen for landing more soldiers, and as a shelter while they returned fire. The bridge had been taken and was heaving with armed pike men and swordsmen.

Meanwhile, although the crossbowmen's rate of fire was slower than the hail of missiles from the Cornish, it was more deadly. Locals fell, punctured by black crossbow bolts. At the top of the beach and between the huts, boats were overturned and propped up with oars to provide cover for the rag-tag gang of townsmen. From the cottage windows behind, a few archers fired sporadically. Only long range resistance was possible. The Spaniards were professional soldiers, with the equipment to match. Once a sufficient number of pike men had been landed on the beach, the screen of shields was lowered and they charged forward, cutting down a few rash defenders, prompting the rest to run.

He remembered his Dad saying, after any dangerous incident at sea: "There's a time to think and a time to act." The time for thought was almost over. He must do something: he must act. But what had he seen that would help? The galleys were moored, pointing away from the bridge. The nearest was within longbow range, surely? They had expended valuable time on arrival to turn the ships around. Why? It was obvious. The river was deep enough for the draught of the galleys at high or, half-tide, but not at low tide. The moon was full, therefore there were spring tides. He calculated that, despite this, the Spaniards had about four hours before they ran the risk of being stranded. Although they had three shiploads of men, and were more powerful than any defence force the townsfolk could raise now, they most certainly knew that they could not wait for the next high tide, by which time the surrounding countryside would have sent many fighters. He noticed that they had left substantial guard on the ships, too. This was their weak point: threaten the galleys, or their line of escape, and they were likely to retreat. The most vulnerable galley was the single one nearer the estuary, at the wooden quay by his home.

Behind him, at Portbodriggan, he heard the sound of crackling. He turned to the sight of red flames and black smoke spiralling from the familiar rooftops. He was isolated and helpless.

Refugees were climbing and scuttling along all the tracks and roads, heading out of town in every direction. Carts and braying donkeys were strewn across the hillside, abandoned.

What could he do right now to throw off this strange lethargy? He was not useless; he had some skill, some pride. The Cornish were renowned for their wrestling and their archery.

He had reached the point where he was just above the bridge, and the road that led from it. Moving down the slope, he gauged the distance to the nearest galley. The range was quite long, though he had the advantage of the hill. He lifted his longbow, nocked an arrow to the string and drew back in the practiced manner that he had rehearsed over many aching hours since his first "baby" bow was given to him on his sixth birthday. He effected the curious archer's fast dance-like motion of pushing the bow forward with his left hand, whilst bringing it up and pulling the bowstring with the other. Finally, he stepped into the bow to gain full muscular power and an instant smooth release. Each necessary and proven part of the action, learned in detail by trial, advice and error, were merged into a lightning movement. It had to be as no man alive could take the strain of drawing such a war bow for more than a split second. The first shot missed. His second shot was a drop shot aimed at the helmsman; it hit him squarely between the shoulder blades. The man fell and his helmet rolled across the deck. Luck, not skill, he admitted to himself. Exposed on the hillside, he shuddered with fearful exhilaration; a tiny victory. What now?

Something whirred by and struck the slope above him, but he kept moving. His zig-zagging reflected the indecisiveness of his thoughts.

The Spanish were experienced enough to follow a plan, he realised. Apart from the ships' guards, the rest had split into two groups. One would burn and loot the town, and no doubt kill and rape in their excitement and indifference to the population. They would be looking for provisions, but also searching for gold and silver, and indeed, any valuable metal. The churches would be the first to be ransacked; the bell of St. Nicholas Church had ceased its warning toll. Even now they would be cutting the bell loose and dragging it to their ship. The Guildhall would be ransacked for specie. Leather, shoes, boots, cloth, wool, and weapons of all kinds would be passing back to the ships, from hand to hand in a stream. Any man caught in fine clothes would be stripped and tortured to reveal their hidden valuables or, if noble, held for ransom.

Any woman would be hurriedly raped and left as a mark of contempt for the town.

The other group of soldiers had marched off up the principle roads, chasing refugees, gathering dropped valuables and collecting abandoned carts and barrows. At strategic spots, they set-up barricades on the highway and pickets on nearby high-points. Their task was to prevent aid reaching the town.

The white-haired English and Breton speaking cleric, who had questioned him at sea earlier that day, was on the foreshore speaking to some kneeling prisoners whilst their captors hung others from the bridge as examples. Several of the prisoners pointed in the direction of the hidden houses of Shutta and Pendrim, towards the wealth of their betters, hoping in vain that it would save their lives. They were grabbed by the hair from behind; their chests ran red instantly as their throats were cut.

He fired again but could not even see where the arrow went — he would waste no more of his valuable, beautiful arrows. There would be no enemy arrows to pick-up and re-use.

A band of Spaniards formed up and headed for the hidden valley of Shutta, which joined the river a quarter of a mile above the bridge.

Peter was a stunned spectator until he came to his senses and started to think. Shutta was a narrow valley that was easily barricaded and defended — they would have their hands full — so no relief could be expected from there. Pendrym was too far away, and would most probably be supporting Shutta.

The most likely and timely source of help could come from the villages and manors to the west — Trelawne, Hendersick, Plint, or Polperro perhaps? But the Spanish barricades on the road would stop them.

He had attracted attention. As several crossbow bolts whipped by, he retraced his steps uphill and downstream.

Just then, a figure with a lumbering gait scrambled down the hillside at the same time a crossbow bolt buzzed past Peter's ear. Michael, a cobbler, looked petrified. Peter decided right then that *he* wasn't going to be scared. He was pleased to see that his friend carried a longbow too.

"I saw you and went home for my bow."

"Yes, good man. Keep moving, they've got my range!"

"You actually fired at them?"

"It seemed like a good idea."

Another buzz overhead: the crossbowman was making a poor job of adjusting for firing upwards. But the two of them were too little a force to disable a ship, he had to think again.

"Let's go before they send men up here to get us..."

Further up the slope they rested. Some Spaniard had set the small chapel of St. Anne's, in the middle of the wooden bridge, alight. That was a mistake as it would soon threaten the galleys and their moorings.

Michael's eyes flickered red from the reflection of the flames of the town.

"What are we going to do, it's horrible?"

"Follow me. Help will come from westwards, if at all..."

"That's no good for us."

"Let's keep moving this way fast, while I work out what to do."

"I can't get in close to them; I've only got this bow. You saw the range of their crossbows."

"I'm not asking you to go closer. I'm guessing that the single ship at Portbodriggan will have followed the same strategy as the others and barricaded the road up the valley. That's the way that help will come from, I know for sure." He didn't, but this was no moment to undermine what little courage they still had.

They cut through gardens and an orchard, then crawled over the skyline as if hunting deer. Not that they ever had: that would be quite illegal. Peter was gratified to see the Spanish deployed around an array of carts, boxes, small boats and hencoops — all built up into a barricade and draped with nets.

He grabbed Michael's shoulder and pointed: on the high ground to their right were two sentinels, one with what looked like a hand bell.

"We must kill those two at the same time."

"How will that help? There are masses more down there.

Two won't make a difference."

"It'll make all the difference. Trust me, there's no time to explain."

"We'll just draw attention to ourselves."

"Well, what are you here for then, you may as well go! I'll do it myself."

"No, no, I'll do it. I was just asking, that's all."

"When we get closer, you take the one on the right, I'll take the other."

"Right, I take the one on the right, yes got that."

"When I whistle, do it instantly. Got it? And no talking until it's done."

They both nocked arrows and crept closer through the gorse until they dare go no closer. Every moment threatened exposure.

They stood and almost simultaneously, drew their bows and aimed. Michael fumbled slightly. With difficulty, Peter wet his lips and let out a thin whistle.

Michael's target was hit through the neck and fell as if pole axed, still as a log. Peter's wriggled and rolled in agony, snapping the arrow that had penetrated the chain mail of his back. Peter rushed over and trod on the soldier's neck whilst pulling the bag on his shoulder to the front to extract the fish knife. This was different from gutting or heading fish and he was not sure whether he thought of himself and his fear, or his father and his anger, when he stabbed the blade full-length between the neckline of the mail shirt and the throat. There had been four people and now there was just the two of them, their panting and the stillness. Michael was taking great gasps of air and looking at him with mixed horror and relief.

There were no calls from below, they had not been spotted. Next, they heaved the bodies into a sitting position so each leaned precariously against the other. Peter sent Michael back a short distance to the fence of the orchard to fetch some palings. They used these to prop-up the wobbling torsos of their victims. From a distance, it would just look as though the guards had tired of standing and had sat down.

Michael cringed at his sticky fingers and wiped his bloody hands down his front.

Peter and Michael then cut across country to the top of the lane that ran down into Portbodriggan. A few dropped articles marked the trail of the refugees.

The obscure reasoning and guessing of Peter's thinking was vindicated when they saw a body of armed men hurrying down the lane towards them. At their head was an armoured figure on horseback, who reined back warily and glanced at each side of the hedges.

Peter and Michael made their obedience to the man, who they only knew as the Lord of Trelawne, by touching their brows and bowing.

With impatience, Sir William de Bonneville, Steward of Trelawne for the Marquis of Dorset, asked them who they were and what they had seen. Thinking fast, Peter used his bloody knife to scratch a diagram of the attack in the earth of the track. He then explained the deployment of the enemy.

"They've split their forces then, with the smaller part ahead?"

"Yes, Sir."

"So what is ahead?"

"A barricade, which you can get behind if you go around to the left."

"Easier said than done, they'll have guards watching for that."

"Dead guards, we killed them."

"No bravado now." He looked at Michael. "Is this true?"

"Yes, Sir, my Lord. With our bows."

"How many men are we expecting to face?"

Peter was shocked into dumbness for a moment. He didn't know; he had forgotten to count. He tried to visualise the scene from the hill and estimate.

"Hurry, boy!"

"About half the men that you have here?"

The Lord called out an order and a dozen men came trotting along to the front. They were archers.

He addressed Morgan, the apparent captain of the

archers, sternly.

"Outflank on the left — their right — got it. These boys will show you the way and they can help. Don't get seen. When you hear my hunting horn, open fire on their backs while we attack. Once in the town, use your sense. Kill all crossbowmen first. Be sure some of the men kill the galley crew, too. If we get the chance, I want to put it across the river and trap the rest as the tide ebbs. Now go!"

Morgan grabbed Peter by the collar and propelled him forward towards Portbodriggan.

"Lead the way, lad."

Stumbling, Peter squeaked — or so it sounded to him: "Come on! Follow me!"

Some of the archers grinned as they trotted after him, leaving the lane and across the fields, diverting well away from the barricade. At one point in their circuitous route, he could see distant black smoke upriver: Shutta was in flames. All those merchants' fine houses, their wives' fine clothes, their tapestries, all going up in an inferno.

They moved on their haunches through the gorse to a point overlooking the back of the barricade. A few Spaniards were looking up the lane to the first bend, most were lounging about examining and exchanging looted objects, others were smoking long pipes. From a hovel a few yards back they could hear grunts and squealing, but whether from a pig or a captured girl, they couldn't tell.

Morgan compressed his lips, looked at Peter, then shook his head and pointed to the top of the opposite hill.

There were look-out guards there, too. Peter realised how lucky he and Michael had been not to have been detected when they'd killed the two other guards. He hadn't even thought of the possibility of guards being on the other side of the valley. They must have been dutifully watching the lane to the west. Now they had much to distract them: envy at the fun going on below, anxiety about being left behind, and the other two galleys.

There was a danger that the look-out guards on the opposite

slope would glance back and see them. They seemed intent on looking ahead, but would they be distracted long enough? Occasionally, they glanced across the valley towards the river and the bridge. Passing through an apple orchard, the small body of archers were moving fast now. They caught a guard's eye. The two sentinels seemed to jump up and down, hallooing an alarm and clanging a hand bell. Too late.

The Lord of Trelawne had timed his approach perfectly. Before anyone appeared from around the bend in the lane, a hunting horn sounded and Morgan gave a single order: "Now."

His archers started to rain arrows down onto the, quite literally, sitting targets in the lane, each firing at a rate of three or four per minute. More and more fell as Morgan's men descended the slope, closing in on the enemy. Peter and Michael joined in, the firing as fast as they could. It seemed amazing that surprise could paralyse so many of the Spaniards for so long. Hardly an arrow was wasted. Peter barely noticed the attack of the swordsmen, spearmen and poleaxe men on the barricade, which was soon swept aside. Their Lord, astride his horse, burst through, hacking left and right with his bright sword.

Morgan blew a whistle, at which his men ceased firing and turned to him for direction. He pointed down towards the harbour. As their Lord pointed with his sword, the whole raging horde poured down the hill and overtook the wounded enemy, and giving no quarter, except a poniard under the shoulder blade or into an eye socket.

It took a little time to drag Spaniards now hiding in the cottages and despatch them.

Soon the harbour was reached, where they were engulfed in smoke and smouldering ruins. Father Fiddick lay dead, his arms outstretched as if in bloody welcome. They were too late. The opposite eastern bank was ablaze — the Spaniards had done their worst. The galley, lately in harbour here, had escaped to mid-river and was trying to turn towards the sea. Upriver, the twelve arches of the bridge belched flame like dragons' mouths, and the church built in the middle of it blazed like a candle. The other two galleys, having had to quit the bridge, were threatened by the ebbing tide and the weight of their loot. They had embarked all of their soldiers and were making their way downriver for the estuary, too. Beyond the bridge, and unable to cross, were Cornish levies from Shutta, who were hoping to capture any laggards.

Peter shouted at the Lord of Trelawne, "Nailzee Rock!" and got a clump from a passing soldier for his temerity.

"The tide, the sand-bar!" he persisted. The Lord seemed not to have heard. However, he considered for a moment and then, without the least bit of acknowledgment, shouted an order and pointed his sword towards a track that led over the hill towards the sea, to the estuary and — Nailzee Rock.

They could see the Shutta and Pendrym men running along the opposite shore to avoid the smoke from the burning town. A race began. A few lagged to gather spent arrows, the rest forced weary legs to climb the steep hill between them and the sea, hoping to out run the three galleys. Peter and Michael, despite their youth, and without the weight of armour, mail or helmets, were able to keep up with the grown men. Soon they passed between a few houses, across their gardens, and over the hill to the cliff that overlooked the estuary and Nailzee Rock. Across the river, St. Mary's church burned its tower in a corona of flames. The saw the first galley trying to traverse the sandbar at the estuary entrance. The boat was being carried by the ebb tide and the helmsman appeared to be having trouble steering due to the lack of "way", despite its oarsmen heaving and its great sails flapping. Yet this ship was only slightly laden with little loot, along with a much depleted force and crew. Opposite, the men from Shutta and Pendrym stood in the shallows raining arrows, spears and stones onto the ship with little effect. Although they were close, they were firing upwards and kept missing, or hitting the wooden side.

On the Nailzee side, the Cornish spread precariously over the steep slope that ended in a cliff. A few bolder men climbed down to the rocks, trying to disrupt the oars. Soon they were all pouring a steady fire at the cringing men below, conscious of the fact that they must save some arrows to use on the other two galleys. Panic gripped the crew as they argued, and struggled to cast loot overboard to lighten the ship. Arrows, slingshot stones and spears fell like hail onto wood and flesh alike. The brave helmsman, who could neither hide nor move, was struck down and replaced by a cowering figure, who, as luck would have it, was still standing when the vessel, its oars smashing on the nearby rocks, shuddered and slipped over the sand bar and was free.

There was a delay as the following two galleys made their way down the river.

Peter stared at the burning town: "Why?"

A grizzled soldier answered: "Their revenge, lad. Some of us, and the English, take their ships at sea and raid their towns, and…"

"What good will it do now? They've done their worst!"

"Ah! our revenge — a justice of sorts. Think of it as being practical: making Shutta a painful memory for them — a costly victory. A place they will never willingly return to again, nor will they advise any other foreigner to do so either. Now get ready, here they come again!"

The next galley stroked its way towards the waiting Cornish. This one was more heavily laden with troops and loot. Crossbowmen and archers engaged in a battle with one another. Michael was the first casualty with a bolt in the eye; he fell and slithered over the edge. The archers spread out and withdrew to safer firing positions, where their greater rate of fire, the stability of ground underfoot, and firing downwards paid off. The crossbowmen, who were crowded on a rocking boat and trying to fire in all directions at once, impeded by masts and rigging, and the need to fire upwards, were quickly slaughtered.

What had been an easy prize became a pyrrhic victory for the Spanish as, to survive, they had to make the bitter choice of either throwing their considerable booty overboard or being slaughtered.

With all hands rowing and a near empty vessel, they slewed and slid over the sandbar.

The last gaudy vessel encountered a similar fate. On the aft-deck stood the proud Don Pedro el Nino, helmeted and breast plated in gleaming steel, his sword sheathed, and his beard jutting out. A look of disdain crossed his features, as others around him flinched and ducked.

Peter pushed forward and balanced dangerously on the edge of the cliff. He nocked his last arrow to his bowstring and felt no anger, just cold certainty that this was right. This was what he had to do before returning to what would be a completely different life. A hopeless shot, he knew.

He drew, aimed and fired as dispassionately as he would during practice at the butts on Sundays.

Fate is fickle. Just as a father and son's gentle morning's fishing can turn awry, its circle is rarely completed to human satisfaction. The arrow hit Don Pedro in the upper leg. For a few long moments of agony, he was humbled. He suffered the pain of being human and threshed, and swore on the deck in his bloodstained finery. For the first time in his life, he doubted his nobility and his God.

No-one knew it was Peter's arrow, but he did. A professional archer near him bounced up and down yelling, "In the arse! The arse! The arse! Well, nearly."

And then the galley was over the bar and away, leaving Peter with an emptiness and disappointment that only youth and years could eventually dispel.

On the beach, by the hissing stumps of the bridge, there stood a man with a bald head, curtained with long white hair, he was wearing dark ankle-length clothes. He tried to look inconspicuous. He had been left behind. It was close to sunset, perhaps he could hide until darkness fell?

Everyone would either be too busy or shocked to notice him. If only people would understand how he came to be a prisoner of the Spanish. He was English, he could read and write, and he could speak several languages. If he could get through the next few days, perhaps someone would find him useful. Maybe he could find a priest to intercede for him. At that moment, someone shouted; someone else pointed. A crowd gathered and approached him slowly, like a long-watched breaker on a cold sea. In the next few minutes, he was to discover that it was not only the Spanish Dons who were cruel and lacked compassion.

Historical Note

Source: The Victorial of Don Pedro Nino.

Books: *The Unconquered Knight: A Chronicle of the Deeds of Don Pero Niño.* By His Standard-Bearer, Gutierre Diaz de Gamez (1431-1449). Translated and selected from El Vitorial by Joan Evans.
Defending the Island, by Norman Longmate.
There are brief mentions from the same sources in various books about Looe.

Internet: Google search using the phrase "Pedro Nino" or "Pero Nino" and "Cornwall".

The interpretation of the town, "Tache" or "Chitta", where Pedro Nino's first raid took place is disputed. St. Erth and St. Ives, as well as Looe, have been suggested. From their location, I think that this is unlikely as St. Ives and St. Erth are on the North coast, requiring a much longer and more dangerous voyage. It is also much further away from the subsequent ports attacked.

St. Erth would involve sailing into considerably well-defended Fowey harbour, and then along a creek that would commit the galleys to going quite a way inland, with the promise of an exciting return passage. Again, the sequence of attacks is wrong as the records talk of being repulsed from Fowey, which also had a chain boom across the harbour entrance.

Looe was known, at that time, as Shutta, phonically closer to the sound of Chita or Chitta. This name survives in Shutta Lane. Looe better matches the description in the Victorial, with its bridge, creek-like narrowness, the houses and streets that ran down steep slopes towards the river, the sandbar at the mouth and the high ground at the entrance. It is also much closer to the subsequent ports attacked, assuming Nino's galleys were moving up and down the Channel shore with the tide.

It took about four or five years to raise funds to build a new wooden bridge. It was constructed by 1411. Unfortunately, this bridge also burned down in 1436. In its place, a stone bridge with fourteen arches was built. The stone bridge was repaired in the 17th Century, then replaced in 1853, about one hundred yards upstream.

The invention of gunpowder and guns by the second half of the 15th Century meant that enemy ships could not enter ports such as Looe with impunity. The harbour was guarded by small batteries of cannons placed strategically above East Looe beach. Later, as cannon manufacturing improved, longer range cannons were installed on the Wooldown, commanding most of Looe Bay. Hasta la vista, Pedro!

Looe Island

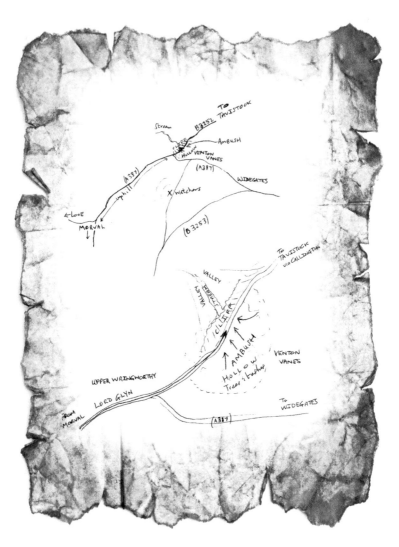

Site of the ambush of Lord Glyn and surrounding
area near Morval

Murder at Morval

1471

On the hill, the watchers shivered, chewed stems of grass and strained their eyes, staring south along the road to Morval. Welkin pointed.

"There, jus' coming up onto the flat."

"Where? Oh yes, I see 'em."

The light of dawn cast long shadows of the travellers on the road from Morval, to the relief of the two watchers on the hill, who'd begun to worry that Sir John Glyn and his entourage had taken another route.

The ambuscade spot was well-chosen. Lord Glyn would be a mile from his manor house at Morval, away to their left. He would be off guard this early in his twenty-five mile journey to Tavistock via Menheniot and Callington. Anyone escaping the attack would likely take an hour to get help. It was nearly a mile long ride to reach Morval, where they would need to gather armed men, then return uphill. They would be far too late. Besides, the watchers would signal to warn of any imminent relief force.

Below, and to their right, their leader Thomas Flete, with the rest of his band, were hidden in trees at the side of the track. At this point, the track passed through a series of bends into a hollow that extended to the right, opposite a small cliff to the left. Ordinarily, this was a suspicious series of landscape features, but it was too familiar and close to Morval for Glyn to think it boded any danger.

A week ago, Welkin, had scouted the place with a disguised Clements, Flete's master. He knew the plan was a good one — the spot a death-trap. Glyn would be surprised, hedged-in, attacked from the flank. His followers would be killed in the attack, or pushed over the cliff.

If things went well, or even, if by some terrible mischance they did not, then Flete and his men would separate and vanish into the surrounding countryside.

Clements was far away, alibis were well established, and false witnesses paid.

Welkin was a trusted confidant of Flete, which was why he had been allocated the vital role of signalling. They had agreed on the point Glyn had to reach before, from behind the cover of an oak, he would wave the piece of red linen that he was currently wringing in his hands in excitement. If he hurried, he could reach the fighting before all the fun was over. Yes, he would descend the hill and join in. He would remember to creep, using cover because, God help him, if he gave the game away — friend or not, Flete had a violent temper when crossed or let down.

Glyn had to be past the point where...

Welkin saw a movement on the road, between Glyn and the waiting Flete.

"Damn fools."

His companion, Jake, spat out a dandelion stalk that he had inadvertently chewed, along with stalks of grass, and pulled a face...

"What? Who?"

"Them down there, lying down behind the hedge. Glyn's got to be past them before we — I — gives the signal."

"They're ours, are they?"

"Of course they are, you winnard. The fools are supposed to stay hidden, not fidget about."

"I didn't even know they were there — what they doing?"

"Well, masters Clements and Flete don't take you into their trust like they does me. Those four are supposed to be hiding down there so they can bring down anyone escaping from the big fight. To stop them getting back to Morval."

They watched intently. Glyn and his fifteen men went past. That part of the trap was ready.

"Are you signalling now?"

☽ ☺ ☾

Flete was calm. He listened, but not for Glyn: his own men watching for the signal from those on the hill would warn him of his enemy, who hopefully was approaching unawares. No, it was a question of discipline. This rough band needed a heavy hand.

They had to be told, asked to repeat what they had been told, and then told again. If they were allowed to drink between an order and its execution, then he might as well have been trying to train cats. He and his sergeants had to check, cajole and punish, or they'd all run the risk of perishing.

Now, he listened for any noises from his men: the clink of metal or the creak of leather. They had been ordered to silence all accoutrements and weapons. Horses were tethered some way away, ready to be brought at five blasts of the bronze whistle that hung on his chest. Nags were likely to whinny or neigh at the smell of other horses.

He'd had a few pointed stakes set in the ground at the bottom of the small precipice across the highway. It was only about forty feet deep at most, but man or horse that fell that far were not going to take any further part.

These trees, this lane, this dust: this was the last place Lord Glyn would see, and if all went well, Flete's eyes would be the last he would ever look into. Waiting in suspense, he hugged his hatred to his heart. Anticipation and glee stoked his excitement. Glyn, with his fine house and proud wife, was an usurper, who, on a change of favour at court, had displaced the Clements family from the lucrative offices of Deputy-Steward of Cornwall that they'd held in Kernow for decades. Flete's patron, Thomas Clements, was out of favour with the King and the political faction of courtiers that had the Royal ear. He and his compatriots were virtual outlaws in their own country. All for a few misdemeanours, customs of the county, that those foreigners in England and London did not respect.

Clements's family, and their trusted friends, were landowning gentlemen and yeoman with tenants and followers, not peasants.

Once he had worn silks, lace, pearls and gold that lit the maiden's eyes with wantonness. He had practiced the arts of war — riding, jousting, swordsmanship and archery — only for excitement, braggadocio and betting. Now he dressed in the black, brown and grey of leather and steel. Nowadays, his skills were deployed in the cause of revenge and self-aggrandisement.

He comforted himself with Clements's reasoning: all that counted down here was force, and who could guarantee peace and collect the King's taxes. The King's favour and lucrative offices could be regained through demonstrating strength, offering fealty and the judicious tendering of a golden gift. If a deal with Clements — reinstatement — was cheaper than enforcing power from London, and the Royal face was saved, all might be as it should and it would be worth the gamble.

He remembered Clements's final sibilant whisper in his ear at yesterday's Liskeard bear-bating: "Glyn must not reach Tavistock, or we are all done for."

☽ ☺ ☾

The going uphill from Morval was slow. Mounted men were followed by pack animals and men bearing pikes, swords and bows, that walked and ran alongside them. Lord Glyn intended to send two outriders ahead once they reached the edge of his lands. He hoped that better days would come from this visit to Tavistock on St Romon's day, the eve of the three-day fair. He would be consulting various merchants and moneymen, and concluding an agreement with the Abbey concerning some of his mining interests. Then, there was that other important matter: soon he would have more armed retainers, veteran mercenaries, men displaced from France. The attacks on his property and person would cease, the perpetrators brought to justice; his wife could sleep in peace.

His steward broke into his reverie.

"It's a good plan. With their foreign connections, we can trust the abbot to recruit real soldiers, glad of employment and a fight. That'll deal with our problems here."

"I hope so. I thought they could not go further than the attack on my person at Liskeard. My wife was mortified by the wound to my face. I feared she would turn from me."

"Never, Sir. Women — I mean ladies — like a decent scar."

"But that wasn't the end of it was it? My poor wife shouldn't have had her house sacked. She shouldn't face insult and the assault of her servants when I'm away. I hope we left enough men for her protection this time. The manor's income will suffer if I keep having to take tenants from their work to guard Morval. It's not fair to them either. Their poor homes and families — although less tempting — are left at risk. I hope all is well when we get back tomorrow."

"Oh, yes, I'm sure it will be, my Lord, and when we return we will be able to take the fight — I mean, of course, justice — to Clements's door."

"I just hope these mercenaries are available, and that we can afford them: no last minute demands for more money."

"The Abbott has negotiated for us, and he is a man of his word."

"Office without might at this barbaric end of the country is meaningless. You'd think that King Edward — God bless him — would be troubled that his authority is flouted down here."

"We'll be back before sunset tomorrow. You'll be pointing out the lights of Morval to the Captain of mercenaries from the hill back there."

"I hope not! If it's before sunset, then it'll be too soon to be burning costly candles or tapers, considering all the expense we'll have signed up for."

The steward turned to survey the small column of pack ponies, their panniers bulging with goods. He counted the lucky few mounted men and the archers trotting alongside.

"Keep close, keep up!"

"You have a fine red scarf. I'd call that a favour from a lady. You kept that quiet."

The steward looked away, uncharacteristically bashful: "Yes."

They were just rounding a bend and passing through a dip, their horses hooves splashing through a stream above a waterfall, while the men on foot leapt from stone to stone.

The sweet song of a thrush suffused the pink dawn.

As if in response, there came one long shrill blast of a whistle.

A tree crashed down on the road ahead of them.

A surge of men hit them from the side with pikes and poleaxes before a single sword of theirs had even been drawn. Palfreys reared and riders fell. One rider, his foot trapped in the stirrup, was dragged, yelling, towards the fallen tree where a pike man skewered him to the ground. Lord Glyn tried to gain control of his charger and failed to calm it in the maelstrom of stabbings and missiles that swept his men towards the cliff. He kicked free of his stirrups and crashed to the ground as his terrified horse, still on its hind legs, toppled and disappeared. Flat and winded, he could not draw his sword, so grabbed his dagger instead. The remnant of his men fought on foot with swords and spears. One of them was standing over him. Few had shields and were hard put to defend themselves. As he tried to rise, a pike was thrust low and straight into his thigh. A rider, he thought his steward, was one of the few still in the saddle, and he fought his way back onto the road to Morval, his horse breaking into a strained uphill gallop.

Cut-off and surrounded on three sides, with their backs to the cliff-edge, Glyn's retainers either made their individual decisions or just fought on desperately as they had no time to think.

One thought that, by jumping over the cliff, he could rely on the treetops to break his fall. He was wrong: he broke his legs and lay just beyond the fallen horse, its hooves threshing the air above his head, his screams joining its piercing neighs.

A few of Glyn's archers, usually so effective, had tried to stand-off and fire into the attackers, but with no distance between them, they were soon overwhelmed.

Within a few moments, Glyn's men were down to half a dozen swordsmen. One attacker sacrificed a spear, piercing one so hard, it carried him out over empty air, before letting go, so it up-ended over the edge. Pole axes took the feet out from under others, who were hacked at where they fell. The bodies were looted and then rolled over the edge. Clements's men competed, casting spears and firing arrows, to prick out any life below.

Alone, Glyn turned and hauled himself onto one knee, lashing out with his dagger with one hand and trying to draw his sword with the other. From each side, pikes stabbed diagonally into the earth behind him, preventing him from joining his men in the shambles of the pit. His weapons were knocked from his hands.

The sudden quiet gradually extinguished the din of clashing metal still ringing in their ears.

Welkin, the watcher, had outpaced his companion and arrived in time to see Flete look around triumphantly at his audience, as though looking for applause to break the silence. It was as if he didn't want to end the moment. His eyes, tempered steel blue by the dawn light, stared at each man in turn.

Lord Glyn, through smashed teeth said, "My men are coming from Morval."

At that moment, a horse was led forward, with the body of a man lain over it, head and arms swing loosely; an arrow pointed upwards from his back.

"It seems not. Time to die."

It was then that Glyn saw a flash of red around the neck of one of the watching men; he mourned his poor steward. Until he recognised the face above. His eyes met the curious, yet indifferent, gaze of his friend.

"You'll all hang! The King will bring you all to justice."

"If we were in England and the King lasts that long, yes. But not this side of the Tamar. I'll have died an old man by then."

"For God's sake, spare my wife and servants, please."

"For now, perhaps. If she sees sense. Now get you gone from this world."

Flete smote the Lord of Morval, cleaving his skull. Blood glittered in the probing rays of the sunrise. With the words, "Hurry up, we must separate and hide 'til we are certain we are safe from discovery," he left his men to complete Glyn's degradation.

His rich raiment was stripped from him. His purse, seals of office, signet rings and jewellery and weapons were carefully gathered and put in a pannier to ensure that all got their fair share. It would do no harm to make this appear to be a robbery, although no-one would be fooled.

With much coarse joking, his body was defiled; his head and limbs were hacked-off and arranged like a crooked cross in the highway. Looking back, to Flete's eyes, the stains and detritus of battle, and the remains, seemed like a ruby revenge shining in the golden rays of the sun. He and his band headed off into the moorland, bloody-armed and tired, but exhilarated at the end of the hunt.

Historical and General Note

The site of the ambush was two and a half miles north of Looe, approximately, one mile north of Morval, on the road to Tavistock (thirty miles away) via Callington. From Morval the road passes up a steep hill to Upper Wringworthy. Here there is an even higher hill to the east where I have placed 'the watchers'. The road then narrows before bending to the right towards Widegates, Hessenford and Plymouth. On this bend there is a road to the left which has all of the appearance of straight on, and this is the old road to Tavistock. As soon as this lane is entered there are two bends with a dips between them, a hollow with a house on the right and a small cliff and valley to the left. It is a verdant area due to the springs and stream. This is my proposed ambush site: the correct travelling time from Morval, on the most direct road to Tavistock and topgraphically an ideal place for a surprise attack.

The displaced Clements seems to have been a local man, at least more so than Glyn, as he seems to have had a greater degree of local support.

Glyn left Morval at 4 a.m, which he would have needed to do in order to reach Tavistock in time to do business. I have speculated on his reason for going there, in light of the series of attacks on his person, servants and house. I have worked out how far he would have reached by the approximate ambush time of 4:30a.m., bearing in mind that not all his retinue would have been mounted, and taking into account the kind of steeds and pack animals used. The long hill up from Morval would have slowed the group. The high hill, now bearing a radio mast, is a superb lookout point. The ambush site is well chosen with its dips and bends and, due to the stream, concealing bushes and trees. Attacked from the right and with a cliff on the left, there would have been nowhere to escape.

The area is called Ventan Vanes. It is hard to determine when this name was first used, and its meaning in Cornish.

Although, it is tempting to see some connection between this name and the Cornish word — "venjans" — for vengeance, it could equally be related to "vent" for an archery butt, or more likely dirty water.

Higher Wringworthy is given as the site of this incident, which occurred on the 29th of August, 1471, near Morval. The sources are: the petition of Lord Glynn's widow, Jane, to Parliament (Rolls of Parliament) and David Gilbert's "History of Cornwall".

Jane Glynn petitioned Parliament for justice and included the words:—

> *"The said Thomas Flete &c. then and there, at four of the clock in the morning, him feloniously and horribly slew and murdered, and clove his head in four parts, and gave him ten deadly wounds in his body; and when he was dead they cut off one of his legs and one of his arms, and his head from his body, to make him sure; and over that, then and there his purse and twenty-two pounds of money numbered, and a signet of gold, a great signet of silver in the same purse contained, a double cloke of muster-de-viles, a sword, and a dagger, to the value of six marks, of the goods and chattels of the said John Glynn, feloniously from him they robbed, took, and bore away."*

Warrants were issued for Clements's arrest, but he was still free in 1476. Although, it is reported that he was executed some years later for some other crime.

This petition is enrolled on the roll of the Parliament summoned at Westminster in October 1472 (12 Edward IV) and prorogued a number of times until January 1475 (Rot.

Parl. vol. VI, pp.35a-38a). It would seem, from pp.3a and 39a that this petition was delivered during the session which lasted from 3 October to 30 November 1472.

The small cliff is currently about 36 feet high, and likely to have been steeper in the 1470s. It is invisible from the road; all that can be seen is what looks like small bushes, which are actually the tops of trees. The small ravine below the ambush site is rather lovely, and when exploring, I saw a bright vermillion red object (bringing to mind the horrible murder that I speculate happened overhead). I rationalised that it was modern junk that had been thrown down from the road. Close up, it was on top of a piece of rotting wood, almost directly under the white flowing water. It looked like four or so large vivid red petals. I took a photograph and later identified it as the fungi Scarlet Elf Cap — quite rare in Cornwall, but rather common in Ireland. A most beautiful thing. Two weeks later it was gone.

Morval Ambush Site

A Cornish hollow lane

The Battle of Braddock Down

1643

When he recognised the lone horseman's face, Henry Killigrew's instinct told him to deny his own name and tell the rider to keep going. It was unsafe to have his history in this year of 1655. The Royalist cause was dead, King Charles beheaded, and Lord Protector — "King Oliver" in all but name — was ruling the kingdom.

James Hedding knew him, but hopefully he was here by chance and not design.

So a night's lodging was granted the traveller. Once Henry's wife had provided a meal, the children had paid their respects to the visitor, and his family had retired, Henry and James sat by the fireside washing an excellent beer around in their cheeks. Only then did James find a way to broach memories of the war.

"You've done well for yourself."

"Just enough to make a reasonable living, but these are hard times."

"For everyone."

"Where are you going?"

"Further west."

Henry briefly speculated whether James was carrying secret despatches to one of the few Royalist strongholds that was still holding out against — or rather being left to starve — by the Roundheads. That would be St Michael's Mount. Or possibly St Mawes Castle, or had that already fallen, he couldn't remember. He didn't really care and didn't want to get involved.

"I think, Sir, that you are a dangerous visitor to have staying."

"One night only. I knew you wouldn't turn me away."

Couldn't, more like, thought Henry.

There was an embarrassed silence, and for a moment Henry wondered if he had spoken his thoughts aloud.

The wind rattled the windows and the flames of the fire danced an erratic jig before James broke the silence.

"Some of us have to keep working. I just want what you've got. You did well."

"I just seized the opportunity and moment, and used the abilities that I had. I was lucky."

James rummaged in his saddlebag and withdrew a small pamphlet.

"I thought you'd like to hear the official Royalist version of the Battle of Braddock Down."

Henry knelt close to the fire to read part of a letter by Royalist Grenville's, quoted in the pamphlet, which read:—

"I had the van and so following prayers in the head of ever division I ledd my part away, who followed me with so good courage, both downe the one hill and up the other, that it strook a terror in them, while the seconds came up gallantly after me, and the wings of horse charged on both sides. but their Courage so faild them, as they stood not our first Charge of the foot but fledd in great disorder, and we chast them divers miles".

A twisted smile and a sniff from Henry:

"Let them take the glory; I prefer the gold."

"Do you remember the night I met you near the bridge? Scared! I thought that any minute I would outdo my horse at shitting. But you were as cool as the river water."

"I was a scout and had every reason to be there. You had miles to go in the dark." "What would you have done if we'd been caught by a Parliamentary patrol? Could you have explained that away?"

"If anyone had found us, I would have — reluctantly — shot you dead as an enemy: a perfect explanation."

James gulped down the last of his beer.

Henry smiled grimly:

"Time for bed, I think, you'll need to start early. Bridget will leave you some vittals in that cloam oven there."

"Thank you."

"How did you know that I was here?"

"Our masters keep note of where we are just in case they need us — regardless of whether we're employed by them."

"You're playing a dangerous game. A game that is already lost. Cut your losses and your ambitions and keep your head down. Find yourself a good woman. Either settle somewhere where you are not known, or surround yourself with people you trust."

"That's your advice is it?" a glint of steel in his eye.

"Yes, I wish you well. But one more thing: don't return here."

James settled by the fire, watched by Henry's hounds.

Henry retired to his warm wife and bed, a dagger within reach.

And as he lay there, vivid memories of his youth and the heady days of the Civil War swarmed into his mind. Fore Street, Liskeard, Cornwall, in 1642 the first year of the war, just before the first Battle of the war…

🌙 🌕 🌒

Henry Killigrew was surprised to find himself proud and thrilled to be in the throng of soldiers marching through the main street of Liskeard. The tramping of boots, the jingling of harness, the clip-clopping of horses' hooves, echoed through the streets as the Parliamentary army of Lord Ruthven made its way through the sullen crowds, who were pressed back against the walls of the houses. No, not sullen perhaps, he thought, more curious and calculating. There were a few black clothed puritans standing apart, preaching from Bibles with the occasional "Hallelujahs!".

His own Cornish people, more catholic by tradition, and therefore more Royalist in the face of the dour, fanatical Roundheads from that strange country across the Tamar, remained silent. Once, someone spat on the ground. An act that was corrected with a swipe from a heavy riding gauntlet, just in case insolence had been intended.

Oh! the power and immediacy of the military. Yes, he owned that he felt a flush of importance, until a familiar face at the wayside winked at him. For a moment, fear overwhelmed his usual cockiness.

This march was a show of strength. Soon, most of the ordinary soldiers would be camping in the fields and heath around the town. Liskeard was too small to billet all of these men. The commanders, officers and elite regiments would find forced accommodation in the townspeople's houses. The ruined castle would be utilised for some horse lines.

Would he be camped, and have to sleep, next to a midden in a rainy meadow? Not at all: he would be here, close to the — admittedly sparse — delights of the town. For the moment, he was important and had the ear of the colonels and generals. He was familiar with the land, he knew the English language, as well as Cornish, and he knew the value of gold from both sides.

From his horse he looked into the middle distance, avoiding what he knew were more than just a few looks of hatred from the bystanders.

It had been a smart move to volunteer his services to the Parliamentarian leader, Ruthven, in Tavistock. The approach had been difficult though. He had been quizzed on his knowledge of the roads and highways of Cornwall by Colonel Carew, before ever glimpsing Ruthven. That first interrogation by Carew had been a trick: there were hardly any roads in Devon, and Cornwall was much worse. Although, there were lanes and bridleways for horses and donkeys. Goods were moved in panniers on packhorses, in small carts, or by boats down rivers, or by sea. Henry knew the wrong answer the Colonel was looking for: good roads to carry cavalry, soldiers marching six abreast, accompanied by heavy artillery and wagons. It was an answer that would have had him buffeted and booted down the stairs in an instant.

Unlike most of the officers, Henry knew that Colonel Carew was a local man. So Henry told the truth. He had lived and played amongst the narrow, hollow lanes around Liskeard as a youth. He knew the secret ways, the woods, hills and bogs — if a scout was required, he was their man. He posed as the black sheep of the Killigrew family: an anti-catholic hater of the King. A resentful younger son of a younger son, jealous of his illustrious relations inheritance. On the way to Liskeard, he had joined in the despoiling of some of the "vile idolatry" in the churches that they passed.

Soon he was considered a good pious fellow and valued for his droll stories and mockery of the Cornish commanders, as well as the army that opposed them. It was all going to be easy. The Royalists were drunken, fornicating fools leading a reluctant rabble of peasants.

Compared with Ruthven's artillery train, the enemy "only had tiny guns that were as small as their pricks, mere harquebuses set on wheels."

Henry recalled his recruitment by the King's intelligence service, and the potential difficulties of what they'd asked of him. The most perilous part was the communication of his progress, the route and details of Ruthven's advance towards the Royalist army at Boconnoc. He could not ride there. However, he had a contact in the town, through whom he could agree a rendezvous point, somewhere midway, with an agent from Boconnoc.

That raised the problem of the Roundhead cavalry. They rode far and wide on reconnaissance. There was a possibility that they could catch him at a compromising meeting, or discover information that would contradict the view he wished to paint in Ruthven's mind.

The other problem was the other scout who had been engaged: he was genuine.

After a few days of occupation by the Parliamentary army, Liskeard folk were furious at the outrages imposed by this alien army. A curfew was announced, bull-baiting and fairs were banned. Fines were levied on Royalist families and property confiscated. Normally, the ordinary people would have been unconcerned at their better's misfortunes, but in these circumstances, anything that affected the master's pounds, also affected his tenant's pennies, and their children's bread. Worse, the soldiers, despite their religious devotion, took liberties with their wives and daughters. By popular opinion, they were prating hypocrites, and were hated more than the French or Spanish.

That evening, a lowly corporal was sent to summon Henry to the commander's lodgings in Tregassowe House. He was not good enough for an invitation to supper, he noted. His presence was required to complement the very crude and inaccurate map, the army's only guide to the county, with his local knowledge. Thus, Henry hoped to influence their plans. Ruthven outlined his strategy, pointing with a gloved finger to a point on the map that was five miles to the west.

"Our intelligence — from letters that we have intercepted, reports of spies — tell us that Hopton and Grenville and the Royalist army are at Boconnoc House. Their cavalry is at Lanreath, but riding far and wide. It looks as though our best plan would be to march along the only real road, the highway between Liskeard and St. Austell, branch off at St Braddock Church, and then travel the short distance, due south into Boconnoc Park, and attack. This should be the fastest route, and it would be easy going for the artillery. Does anyone have any comments?"

Colonel Fiennes moved his hand along the proposed route of attack, "We'll be visible for miles, it's mainly open heath. There will be no element of surprise. We'll also be at a disadvantage if they move out and attack us there — they have more cavalry, remember. We'll also be slowed down by our artillery."

"In which we hold the advantage."

"Only if we can get the enemy in a fixed position — such as in Boconnoc, which they must defend — and then deploy it."

"It's a long way to Boconnoc for slow-moving artillery though. We wouldn't arrive before the afternoon, even if we weren't harassed on the way."

Henry had the inkling of an idea. He listened to the argument raging back and forth, biding his time until a moment of quandary was reached:

"Begging your leave, Sir — My Lord. Will you hear a humble scout who, although he knows nothing of military matters, knows the byways hereabouts?"

"Speak up, but be sharp and to the point."

"That main highway to St. Austell is not the only way. As I see it, you need a concealed way to get to Boconnoc, one that will also mask the sound of moving artillery, yet broad enough to carry them."

"What? You're telling us not to use the broadest mapped road available?"

"Oh no, do use it. Send the cavalry along there as a diversion: lots of flags and flashing breastplates and trumpets. They will think it is the vanguard of the whole of our army. Spread out on the heath adjoining the road, they will have no visibility of what lies behind the screen of cavalry. Would that work, Sir?"

"Possibly, with some military principles applied. But what about the rest of the army, how are they going to advance? This isn't a bunch of yokels going to the fair."

"I know the secret hollow lanes that follow the folds of the hills."

"Squalid gutters!"

"No, Sir, they have been used by locals for centuries. Unlike the main highway, which is much-used by folk who come from far afield, who churn it up as they avoid the potholes and quagmires made by previous travellers," — here Henry waved his head from side to side — "such that it meanders this way and that from one year to the next. The hollow ways are just as good, if not better! They are broad and high-hedged, passing through gentle, wooded hills that would — no will, with God's grace — conceal an army! Look!" Seizing charcoal and paper, Henry sketched the byways that lay to the south of the main highway.

"Those lanes? What about mud, their width, the distance, and the rivers and streams to be crossed?" Pemberton, the other scout cut in.

"And even if they get out onto the open heath close to Boconnoc, where is our cavalry?" Ruthven queried.

"Please. One at a time, gentlemen, and all will be answered."

Henry counted off the objections on his fingers. "I've measured the axle width of your largest culverin: the lanes are wide enough. Locals don't want paths that lead nowhere: there are bridges over the few streams. Mud? well the lanes are well metalled with stones and flints, same as the stonewalls supporting the hedges that border the lanes. Also, look out of the window, winter is hardly over, the ground is hard. The distance: that's less. Check the map. My proposed route is south of the highway, as is Boconnoc, so it is more direct."

"But the cavalry?"

"Well, for the infantry and artillery to get all the way to Boconnoc, it must start early, in the morning mist. The cavalry, making a big hullabaloo, would start on the main highway an hour later. Fairly slowly though, as though screening a slower moving army behind. As the former debouch out of the lanes onto the heath — a complete surprise for the enemy — the cavalry join with them. It's just a matter of timing."

"A surprise, eh? What if the Royalists see us in the lanes?"

"In the lanes, we are concealed, and the rumbling of the artillery is muffled."

"You said all that."

"Because the two parts of the army are moving in parallel, the cavalry is screening us. No enemy can sight us from the north side. The south side is screened by woods and the many streams flowing into the River Looe. We could be seen from the end of the lane if it were straight, but it isn't. It is uphill and down dale, with many bends."

"It sounds very risky to me," barked another voice. "What if they are guarding these approaches?"

Henry waved his hand in acknowledgement: "That is very unlikely. What army would advance slowly through lanes when there is a broad heath they can pass over at speed?"

"We should at least check: send a patrol."

Henry had anticipated this question and was ready to provide the answer should no-one else do so, but there was no need. With the Commander present, everyone was anxious to be noticed. As if on cue, a gauche fellow at the back contributed: "Not a patrol! Too much noise. A single man, send this fellow, the scout."

Henry nodded. There were general sounds of agreement, that turned into laughter as "Gauche" continued with: "And if he doesn't come back, we'll have our answer!"

Henry drew his fingers across his throat and grimaced, joining in the fun.

A sterner voice cut in: "What if the worst happened and we were detected? We would be trapped in hollow lanes, walled in. And how can we communicate with the cavalry during the advance?"

"It's not hollow lanes all of the way. But usefully, it is on the higher ground, where we might otherwise be seen."

Ruthven pointed at the sketch map: "There are two bridges, here and here, so we could retreat and defend those if necessary. There are some crossroads, which will allow a rider to carry messages between the two columns. In extremis, those same roads would allow us to go north and rejoin the main highway and our cavalry."

Murmurs of agreement and doubt, frowns and smiles, filled the room as Ruthven brought the meeting to a close with:

"That's the worst case. Think of the best case, Sirs. Imagine the effect of such a surprise attack on the enemy. Well, it seems that we have the bones of a plan. You do your scouting tonight and report back by eleven o'clock. If all is well, we advance before sunrise tomorrow. As for the rest of you, put all into preparation, you know your duties. I bid you all a good afternoon, gentlemen."

☽ ☯ ☾

There was still time for Henry to visit the churchyard and head left through the lych-gate to find the tenth grave. This was a pre-arranged meeting, set at the same time every day, which he could utilise if required. After an uncomfortable half an hour wait smoking a pipe, he was, in turn, found by a tall, cheerful chap who he had been told was the gravedigger. It was the same man from the crowd who had winked at him. He didn't have time to ask how he'd known who he was. There were other people in the distance amongst the tombs, and a few bonfires. In a low voice he swiftly passed on his verbal message: he needed to meet a contact from Boconnoc to pass on Ruthven's plan of attack. It was too important to be trusted to paper. The rendezvous would be at the second bridge of the hollow lane route that he was due to reconnoitre that evening. To ensure that there was no misunderstanding, he added that this was the first bridge to the west of the old, standing cross at the crossroads between East Taphouse and Duloe track. Disconcertingly, the man smiled and nodded throughout, leaving him no impression that he'd actually been heard, nor of any intelligence. Henry made the gravedigger repeat the message three times and gave the time of the meeting: nine o'clock that evening. Again, he made the man repeat the time three times. And the same for the sign and countersign: the challenge, "Who there goes?" and the reply: "A simple priest". Followed by the whole message.

He ended with a question: "How long?"

The gravedigger looked up at the sky and the weather-vane of the church: "Have no fear. Within the hour."

How the message would be passed so quickly, Henry did not know. He suspected it could only be by carrier pigeon.

☽ ☯ ☾

Quietly, the local priest's wardrobe was looted, and he selected a more modest beast than his army horse. Not unarmed though: he stuck two horse pistols uncomfortably into his belt and wore a sword. This was not unreasonable for a priest travelling at night, in dangerous times, to visit a sick parishioner.

His saddlebags held a bible — the doctrinally correct version for a Royalist — and a hot broth well saddled in rags and straw. It was only at the last minute that he remembered to ask for tonight's password.

He followed the exact route that had been planned for the army's advance the next day. Down the steep Old Road, passing through several pickets. They had been warned and only pretended to question him. As the last lights were left behind, he felt very alone. Soon he was riding through a cold tunnel of ferny dry stone walls and towering arches of hedge.

The comfort of a full moon undimmed the way. Occasionally his mount stumbled on the uneven ground, bouncing him around in the saddle — this was not a horse for a quick getaway.

He travelled uphill for a stretch. Ahead lay a brighter patch of moonlight where the crossroads broke the high sides of the lane. He could see the silhouette of the ancient stone cross and dismounted. Leading his horse by the reins he carefully led it to the track crossing, pausing and peering both ways to look for movement. An owl swooped along the track. Rustling disturbed the hedges. A fox holding something in its mouth stood and stared at him before darting on its way. The denizens of the night were going about their lives unalarmed. He led the horse quietly across the crossroads and, with the aid of a gate, remounted. The lane swallowed him again as he descended into a dark wood. All his senses were alive and he found himself holding his breath. The moonlight made little entry here. Soon he heard something faint, and almost musical. A glittering in the gloom, and then the dark bulk of the small bridge. He rode forward carefully. Suddenly there was movement from the side of the bridge and a mounted figure splashed out of the water. "Who there goes!" He went from startled to relieved and took his hand away from his pistol butts and replied:

"A simple priest."

"You were a bit slow there."

"You idiot, springing out like that. I could have discharged a pistol. Let's get on with this."

"Let's get off this track. Follow me along the stream, it's quite safe. I've ridden it to check."

Although Henry did not find this reassuring, he rode down the shallow bank at the side of bridge and around a bend, heading downstream. If they dismounted now, they'd be fairly secure from sight or sound of their exchange being detected. Crouching under the bank, his boots beginning to leak icy water around his ankles, Henry felt into his pocket and hesitated.

"First things first, the passwords for the next two days: that's tomorrow and the day after?"

"Er, 'Endymion', then 'Falstaff'."

"And the response?"

"I don't remember. That'll be enough. Now come on, where's the message?"

Henry withdrew a large black kerchief, tied with a loose knot, from his pocket.

"Here."

A small bright light dazzled Henry, illuminating a long, gaunt face with a wart on one nostril and long fair hair.

"Put that out you fool!" he hissed, blowing at the lantern in a vain attempt to dowse it.

A shutter on it clicked shut. All Henry could see was darkness and a big blob of after-image obscuring his vision.

He swore and nearly dropped his precious kerchief and its contents.

"Well, come on what's the message," the irritatingly chirpy voice started again.

"I'm not telling you. I don't know where all of the Parliamentary patrols are; you might get captured and tortured."

"Oh! Thanks."

"I'm giving you the message in this kerchief. Don't squeeze it."

"What's in it?"

"Horseshit."

"What!"

"Horseshit. The message is writ small and sewn into leather, concealed in horse manure."

"What the hell for?"

"Keep the kerchief in your hand. If you're about to be captured, then drop the horse dung. In the darkness, it won't be seen."

"And if it is."

"It's ordinary horseshit on the ground. Who's going to query that?"

"It smells. I hope the message isn't shit, too."

"Look, you know what you've got to do. Do it! I'm going."

This was met with more muttering and grumbling.

Henry remounted, with more difficulty than he wanted his compatriot to see, and turned his horse back up the stream. He listened and watched carefully before bursting up the bank into the lane. As he hurried back the way he had come, he was filled with hysterical laughter at this encounter. The kind of sense of silliness that only young men in deadly danger experience.

☽ ☯ ☾

With loose equipment and boots well wrapped, and fuses detached from muskets to avoid accidental discharges, the infantry trudged out of Liskeard. At the bottom of the hill the artillery train joined the end of the column. Four culverin of different sizes, and half a dozen smaller cannons were hauled along by all kinds of steed, ox and men. The wheels slid and lurched, sometimes even turning on the uneven ground. Wagons with cannonballs and powder followed.

Precautions had been taken to prevent any signalling from Liskeard in the direction of the Royalists. The church tower and other high buildings were manned by soldiers. There was a curfew in place until well after dawn. Later, all civilian movement out of town would be enforced by pickets — violently if necessary.

Progress was steady but muddy; the lanes dripping with dew. The infantry were told to trail their pikes whenever it was thought that their height would overtop the hedges. In the confined space, despite the pikemens' expertise, considerable tripping of feet and tumbling occurred.

Generally, all went to plan. Although, the artillery tended to get stuck at times. Then again, it did not need to be at the front of the column when they eventually debouched onto the open heath.

Just over two hours after the infantry's departure, the cavalry started out along the main highway from Liskeard. The timings had been adjusted in response to mounted messengers reporting progress along the hollow lanes. The cavalry spread out as widely as possible, across the highway and its surrounding heath. Flags were flown and trumpets sounded behind them, while small groups of men on foot played fife and drum. It helped that they were advancing on Boconnoc from the east, with the rising sun dazzling their opponent's view. It was pleasing to Ruthven that, to his left, his infantry column in the low landscape were invisible. Henry knew this as, freshly mounted, he rode between the columns. His intelligence was being used by the commanders to co-ordinate the advance. But what if the idiot of the night before hadn't got through? Henry was worried that the Roundheads' plan — his plan — might actually work.

Of course, it could not. Soon the infantry and artillery were strung out over several miles of lane, with the artillery stuck at various bends and bridges. Their progress was not improved by following the tracks of thousands of boots. Branches were torn down and laid across boggy parts to support the wheels.

Finally, the infantry saw the light at the end of the tunnel: the open heath. Henry, by this time on foot, was at the head of the column. Along with Pemberton, he was sent on ahead to scout. Together they walked cautiously uphill, the last one hundred yards of shadowed lane. Pemberton was obviously expecting the crack of a musket shot musket at any moment.

Playing along, Henry crawled out onto the sunlit heath to scan the terrain from side to side.

He saw gorse and a few pieces of agricultural land separated by hedges and dry stone walls. To his right was a valley, and another hill parallel with theirs.

"We're nearly there. Ahead, a bare half a mile away, is Boconnoc. You stay here while I creep along the hedges to see what I can see."

Pemberton was only glad to oblige: out there, on the bare heath, a man on foot was sweet meat to the flashing swords of enemy cavalry.

Henry darted away, running from gorse bush to hedge and hedge to wall, until he was out of sight. Then he broke into a run and ran, and ran. He had no intention of returning; but he would watch.

He heard the drumming of hoof beats. The Roundhead cavalry had surely not arrived yet? Would they cut him down? Or the Royalist cavalry, come to that? A man on the ground was like a mouse to a cat for dragoons.

Grenville was a good as his word. They had watched out for him. A rider, leading a spare mount, was racing towards him. He had rarely been as pleased to see someone, even if it was just the gaunt, wart-faced messenger from the previous night. The idiot could certainly ride though.

Despite his bursting lungs and hammering heart, Henry was in the saddle in a moment.

His saviour leaned over.

"Quickly! the battle is not over yet."

They rode well out of musket shot and reined in.

"My thanks."

"Uhmm… Idiot am I?"

"My apologies for last night. Heat of the moment."

"Fool, eh?"

"No. Really, really sorry. I am Henry Killigrew at your service, Sir."

"Humble apology accepted. I am John Hedding — let's go watch the entertainment!"

And with that, the two young men rode to a high point on the opposite side of the valley, from the Roundhead infantry column.

Already, they could hear the explosive cracks of gunshots and the clash of steel coming from the east where, Hedding told him, the Royalist cavalry were charging the Roundhead cavalry. The rat-a-tat of drums, the squeal of fifes and the blare of trumpets changed to a brief cacophony of distress before ending. Henry could imagine the players being struck down by sword and hoof. From this distance, all he could see was a blur of smoke, movement, flashes of sunlight off breastplates and swords, and the falling of coloured flags. Then the mass diminished and dispersed back along the road to Liskeard… all bar a breakaway group that, split from their fellows, shattered and broken, escaped west along the road to Lostwithiel.

"They were never going to be a problem," Hedding observed.

"Look, the infantry are coming out onto the heath. If they get their superior artillery out, we're finished." He peered nervously over his right shoulder towards Boconnoc.

"Trust Grenville. Watch."

Over the brow of the hill to their left, an army appeared, deploying threateningly to flank the Parliamentarians pouring onto the heath.

"Wow!"

"That's Hopton. There's more."

Trumpets sounded nearby and then far off, as though the sound was echoing.

Further along the hollow lanes, and out of sight, another battle sounded.

Hedding pointed: "We'll see better from up there, from the left wing of our army. We've played our part; we can just watch now."

"Our part? Our part? You cheeky scoundrel. I set all of this up for Grenville to exploit."

"Come on."

A circuitous route took them up the hill and along the back of the Royalist army to its left wing.

The highway lay behind them, but parallel to the army. As they observed, they saw some of their cavalry trotting back through the debris of battle.

To their left, the battle along the lane seemed to be where, for a short distance at least, it passed between a slope and a bog. A Royalist attack down the slope was breaking the passing Roundhead column and was pushing the Parliamentary soldiers into the marshy ground, splitting the head and tail of the army. Panic was setting in. The soldiers pushed forward and backwards, crushing those ahead and behind. Those that could not go back, or forwards, scrambled out of the lanes and away from the conflict.

At the front, the portion of Roundhead infantry on the heath were trying to make some military sense of their predicament. Both sides sent skirmishers forward.

"He's waiting. Grenville, he's waiting," enthused Hedding.

Henry wasn't going to ask why but guessed that, with the Roundhead army split, Grenville was waiting for enough of the army to be on the heath to warrant a worthwhile attack.

A company of Royalists moved aside and a cannon appeared. It fired instantly, with a sonorous boom echoing along the valley.

As if this was a signal, a great yell went up from the Royalist right and they charged down the hill and up the other side chasing the Roundhead skirmishers, who were caught out and began running for their lives. The Royalist infantry arrived with enough breath to drive the enemy back and partly block the end of the lane. The part of the cavalry that had returned, swept along the back of their own army and down the right flank, terrifying the Roundhead foot soldiers on the heath, and completed the bottling-up.

It was as over as checkmate in chess.

Roundheads crouched, their hands over their heads, begging for mercy or clambered out of the lanes, running into the woods, or across the heath, away from the battle.

The hooves of galloping horses behind him made the very cautious Henry realise that he had been remiss. Hurtling towards him was a breakaway company of enemy cavalry. He saw a bright yellow flag with four black lions diagonally across it. With it was a snarling figure in a yellow buff coat adorned with red ribbons, holding a raised sword that was aimed at Hedding.

He turned his horse and fired his pistol; he knew not where. Yellowcoat's horse went down as the sword point missed its mark and cut across Hedding's shoulder blades. More horses fell, to the sound of neighing and men swearing. In the confusion spurred by the danger, Henry grabbed the reins of Hedding's horse and manoeuvred both mounts out of the turmoil. He felt a jarring slice open his right cheek, the shock of which urged him on. Then the hot wetness of blood ran dripping from his chin.

A trumpet blared, followed by cheers and the beat of hooves approaching. Some of their opponents had ridden on, while others paused. The man who had dismounted was Carew. Ruthlessly, a sergeant pushed a trooper off of his horse, allowing their fallen leader to quickly mount. With a look of hatred toward the now too distant Henry, Carew and his men swept away just in time, pursued by a blood-thirsty pack of Cavaliers trampling the fallen trooper.

Hedding, mouth gaping, gulped: "God, that was close. Thank you. Thank you. You saved my life. I thought I'd be spitted on his sword."

"Yes, I saved your life and don't you forget it!"

"He got me though, am I wounded?" he said, peering back over his shoulder.

"No, but I got cut."

"Where? Oh, yes, nothing to worry about, I reckon."

Hedding drew his sword: "Anyway, we're missing all the fun. Let's go hack a few rebels! For the King! For the King!" and he galloped off to join in the massacre of the fugitives. Henry's heart wasn't in it so he remained. His face burned, it was as if he could taste the steel of the sword blade in his mouth. He remembered his own fears of the past few days and did not begrudge anyone their life. The tension of the last few hours had left him exhilarated and exhausted.

Later, when all fighting spirit and defiance had gone from Ruthven's army, Henry took a very slow ride along the lanes, holding a pistol for security. It was pitiful and, to a large extent, a consequence of his own work. Not by swordsmanship and courage, but by scheming. The looting, murder and taking for ransom going on around him could not be interrupted without risking a sword in the gut. It was only thanks to the Bible and the church that any mercy was shown. Sometimes, men thought of their own families and empathised with the beaten, thus sparing them. Others could only end the terror they had experienced by killing one of the "things" that had caused it.

And here, near one of the bridges and the steep hill that led down to it, was some of the wealth of the City of London: the pride of the Roundhead army — its artillery. Abandoned and un-spiked, it was worth more than gold to an army fighting a war.

Beyond, some dutiful sergeant had spilled much of the gunpowder down the track, to spoil it.

The army chased the fugitives into the woods, and along the highway and lanes, towards Liskeard. Here the inhabitants grabbed kitchen knives, working tools and farm implements, and took their revenge.

But Henry had had enough, for three reasons. It was a long, crowded way back to Liskeard. His face was still bleeding. And he suspected that the planners, spymasters and commanders would be loath to exchange the relative comfort of Boconnoc House for the delights of Liskeard. They would leave their underlings to chase the rebels out of Cornwall, and use the time to write despatches and letters to their wives instead.

He turned his horse. By evening, he had retraced his steps and continued on to Boconnoc. Following the victory, the sentries guarding the estate were extremely slack and he was only asked for the password once. An alleged physician saw to his cheek and patched it up. He then put his coat back on so that the darkening stains from his copious bleeding were still evident.

Next, he went through the obsequious necessities and hierarchical stages of approaching his spymaster. The great hall was full of drunken gentry, unkempt and only recently relieved of their armour. He knew that only at this moment, would his part in the battle and his knowledge be valuable to those despatches, letters, anecdotes, and tales of daring composing. Gratitude is short-lived, so now was the moment. He could not see Sir Ralph Hopton, but Grenville, well-refreshed, thanked God for the outcome of the battle:

"What a great and Christian victory it has been. Cornish soldiers have shown great mercy and given quarter again and again. The number of dead is low."

Henry recalled the swords rising and falling on the fleeing army.

Grenville was only counting the gentlemen who had fallen, not the peasants and tenants who had been forced to follow them to war.

His own master introduced him and encouraged him to share his role in the battle, to great laughter at the Parliamentarians' gullibility. Henry was very careful to underplay his own actions and laud the bravery and dash of his betters. His bold form of deference — soldierly bowing and saluting — earned him their good opinion, if not respect. He added, "Unfortunately for me, Sirs, as my face has been seen by so many rebels, it is unlikely that I shall be able to serve His Majesty in this capacity again."

"And now, marked," a voice said, referring to his new scar. To his amazement, before he broached the awkward question of payment, a tankard was heavily banged on the table and several gold coins were flung in his direction. More red-faced cavaliers followed this example. With wide arms, he swept the coins towards him and poured them into his hat until it hung heavily from his two hands that gripped the brim. There was more than he had dreamed of; better than a miserly amount that his mentor had carefully counted out. When his luck was running, Henry knew when to run.

A lost battle, his army routed, Ruthven pondered the draft of his report to Parliament. To the point and no excuses was his way, but let them read between the lines to intuit his difficulties. Concealment in the lanes and a feint to the north had seemed a viable plan of action. Had that scout led him astray? Had he been working for the Royalists? He had disappeared, even though, based on the roster, his pay was in arrears. And he had vanished — not unusual in a battle though — just before they were ambushed. But stick to the known facts, not fanciful explanations, especially ones that would make him look like a fool. He turned to another list and made a mark.

To be sure, Killigrew rose early to wave his guest off. Hedding leaned from the saddle: "I forgot to tell you last night. This hiding away is all unnecessary. We captured some rebel papers later on. You were important enough, or expensive enough, to make it onto the official Parliamentarian lists. I've seen it."

"So? All the more reason to lay low."

"But you are dead! For some reason, Ruthven marked you so on the casualty list. I can't think why!"

His laughter faded into the mist as he rode away.

Historical Background

Braddock Down was the first battle of the English Civil War.

Fatalities in the battle are recorded as low, but that may be simply due to the fact that only gentry and landowners were counted.

I believe that a battle re-enactment at the traditional Boconnoc site drew comments from the participants, those who'd researched the battle closely, that it could not have been the correct battle site as the topography did not agree with contemporary accounts.

The Ordnance Survey "moved" the battle site from the grounds of Boconnoc eastwards, to a triangle of land delineated by a triangle formed by two roads, the A390 and the B3359, and a lane. This move was based on a case put forward by a Mr Wilton (now deceased, and not, incidentally, of nearby Wilton Farm) on the basis that the former site did not match contemporary evidence, nor the distance stated. An army approaching from Liskeard could not have travelled the stated distance in a morning.

In my opinion, the battle site may have been even further to the east. The subsequent re-siting caused a certain amount of embarrassment to the authorities as the Connonbridge Waste and Recycling site now occupies a large part of the probable site.

Close by, to the south-east, an old map shows "The Widowpath", which may be related to the battle, suggesting it was the path taken by fugitives, or just a path by which coffins were conveyed to Pinnock Church. To the east is Culver Wood, which sounds suspiciously like the old words for guns and artillery "culverin" and "calliver". And, it's in the right place for an artillery train that was following an army along the lanes, and was later captured. Nearby, "Connonbridge" is on the route I have suggested; could it have been named "Cannonbridge", originally? I have seen it called the latter only once, in a legal document concerning a "messuage" in the area, that also referred to the "Queen's highway". This would have to be Queen Anne to be after the date of the battle but this is unproven. So, this is doubtful, and "Connonbridge" is probably correct, possibly referring to the Cornish Saint Connon.

What attracted me to the story was the very different versions of events given by the winners and the losers: basically "our spirit and bravery won the day" versus "we were misled and ambushed".

As for Ruthven's misfortune with scouts, he might have been comforted when Hopton appeared to have suffered a similar misfortune a few months later. At Sourton Down Hopton was ambushed, whilst on the March, by Major General James Chudleigh. Possibly, another disaster caused by unreliable scouts.

Chinese coin and top section of navigational dividers
found near *The Flying Wulf*'s wrecksite

Cannon from *The Flying Wulf*,
displayed outside Looe Museum

Hartman's Luck

1691

Moritz Hartman, Governor of Tranque — the first trading post of the Danish East India Company in India — had not seen this coming. Captain Klein, newly arrived from Denmark on the "Flying Wulf" presented him, without the deference due, with a recall letter ordering Hartman to relinquish his post. The tall, pallow gentleman accompanying Klein was introduced as Christian Porck, the new Governor. Hartman was to extend every aid and courtesy to the interloper. He was also expected to introduce him to the princes of the surrounding lands that traded with the Company, to ensure a smooth transition.

Suppressing his anger, Hartman chose his words carefully and delivered them calmly.

"Why? The usual period," — he had nearly used the word "reign" — "for a Governor is years. These cordial and diplomatic relations with the native aristocracy are not built overnight," Hartman blustered whilst his brain raced — what did they know?

"My orders…" Klein began, but Hartman cut in…

"What have I done to deserve this. Are we not profitable? Have I not served my country loyally? Am I not a Knight of San Marco, too. This is an insult!"

"My orders are to escort you back to Copenhagen where this matter can be resolved. Neither I, nor the new Governor, know anymore."

A long, uneasy pause ensued as Hartman's face, as straight

as he could keep it, displayed indignation, anger, defiance, and then something else. Calm? Sardonic humour at the twists of fate, Klein concluded. This is Hartman the brave, the national hero, also the cunning strategist.

"Of course, I need time to pass my knowledge on to, er..." Hartman gestured towards the new Governor, "and to arrange for us to proceed around the princely courts of the hinterland with due deference and ceremony."

"It is all confirmed. We leave on the return voyage of the *Flying Wulf* in three weeks' time, and I will be in command. All of this is laid down in the third paragraph."

Hartman tapped the letter until its hanging seals swung. "There is some mistake, there must be. This is a plot formed by my enemies."

"That is not my concern, though you have my sympathy. You will see, Sir, that the letter is signed by all of the Directors of the Company — who are on the committee — and formally sealed."

The new Governor thrust his hand out. Hartman had to take it, weighing it distastefully as though it were a dead fish. At last, this long streak of smoked kipper spoke.

"Do stay where you are for now, but please arrange suitable accommodation — for our approval."

Klein and Porck pressed for progress, expecting delaying tactics. To their surprise Hartman was the epitome of bonhomie and compliance. Plans were made, transport arranged and soon they were swaying, perched on ornate platforms on elephants or being shaken in dusty carriages. Sometimes they would transfer to riverboats.

As they journeyed, the heat and the mix of smells — spices, dung, sweat, blossoms — sickened and seduced their senses.

At each court, castle, or temple they stopped at, the colours, the richness of clothes and jewels, the beauty of the women, and the glare of the walls, assailed their vision.

At each destination, Hartman noted that Klein made his excuses and held a private discussion with a prince or a court official or, more often than not, with a Jesuit priest, who were used by each royal family for their numeracy, literacy and language skills.

"Where are you going now, Klein?"

"I have other orders, too. Private letters from the company that I need to deliver personally."

"What about? That I, the Governor — the ex-Governor — shouldn't know of?"

"I don't know either. Perhaps it is intelligence on our foreign enemies in these parts. They are confidential correspondences, for their prince's eyes only."

"Are you not curious? Have you never considered…"

"No, I am paid to obey my orders."

The return journey to Tranque was a silent affair of tiredness, suspicion and tension.

The Captain of the *Flying Wulf* was busy dealing with the customary additions and deductions to the crew and passenger list when docked in a foreign port. A desperate supercargo, employed by the company, followed him like one of the stray dogs infesting the streets, entreating: "God! Please, I've not seen my wife and sons for three years!"

"My commiserations, but the company comes first. You will not have to wait too long. Look at the schedule. Wait and you'll go, fully paid, as a passenger in comfort."

"My wife…"

"I'll give her a letter from you. Anyway, this way you'll get an extra few months with the rather attractive Indian mistress I've heard about."

"A servant, only a servant."

Inevitably, even if a ship docked in Greenland, some of the crew jumped ship, mostly Lascars.

He wanted sailors to crew the ship, not passengers. Word spread and he soon had many volunteers. He signed them up and only realised later that they had mostly come from another ship in the harbour — a frigate, *Venezia* — the ship much sailed by Hartman during his governorship. Uneasy, he enquired further of his bosun, Morten Paulsen.

"I've heard they're very good, well-trained seamen. They have been captained by Hartman on several enterprises against pirates."

"I see. Well, I want to keep as many crew members of the *Wulf* as possible. I brought them with me intentionally, as I know them from previous voyages."

"Fine."

"In fact, I want to lay off as many from the *Venezia* as I can."

"That won't be entirely possible…"

"Why? Why not?"

"Well, you signed-them up…To a legally binding contract. We'd have to pay them something to get rid of them. It'd look bad to the Copenhagen coin-counters."

"I'll risk it."

"Despite the apparent appeal of the homeward *Wulf*, we are still short of seamen anyway. Did we make records of the men that came from the *Venezia*? I don't think we did. We can't just lay off those who signed-up in the past month."

"Well do your best and let me know."

"Can I ask, is this to do with Hartman? Is it going to — er — upset Hartman?"

"What of it?"

"He's a dangerous man to cross."

"Then don't tell him."

"He'll find out."

"That's my problem. I have another service for you: please ensure that this letter gets to the Company directors back home. It's vital and no-one else is to know of it."

"But yours is the next ship home."

"It's a safeguard, in case any misfortune befalls the *Wulf*.

Hartman sat in his suite at the Company office overlooking the harbour, watching the *Flying Wulf* being prepared for sea. He had enquired about its history. The frigate was originally Swedish and had been captured during the Battle of Koge Bugt. Later, the government had gifted the ship to the Danish East India Company fleet, as both a contribution and tribute to the company's promise and success that meant so much to the Danish economy. Obviously, they were luring him back to Denmark for some kind of judicial or disciplinary action. Where had he gone wrong? They must have agents here. Somehow, they knew what he'd been up to. Perhaps it was the fort he had started to build at the river mouth? Or his chance meeting with the pirate, George Naylor? He'd been unable to resist the opportunity of exchanging anecdotes with another adventurer. Unfortunately, the Englishman Naylor was suspected of preying on ships of the Great Mughal. Perhaps, in Copenhagen, this was perceived as a threat to all of the trading posts in India? Perhaps intelligence of his meeting with Naylor had reached home?

A substantial donation had elicited from one of the Jesuit priests that Klein had passed on private letters for the client princes. Not only had he handed letters over, he had taken ones from them, too. That could only be perceived as evidence of his, Hartman's, "conduct" as Governor. So the problem lay with the fact that Klein now had a bundle of at least a dozen letters that must not reach Copenhagen. "The Flying Wulf," he mused, that was something that he had no intention of becoming himself.

🌒 🌕 🌘

Klein called his trusted bosun, Morten, to his cabin.

"I have a what you might call a secret mission. I have a bundle of letters, now wrapped in oilskin, which must reach the directors in Denmark. This is a map of the cargo in the hold. And this is where they are hidden — look closely and memorise the location," he indicated to a container with the points of a pair of navigational dividers, and continued: "Without having to empty out almost the entire hold, they will be totally inaccessible whilst we are at sea. Here is a letter of authority from me naming you as my agent, to ensure you get access to our masters — keep it safe. If anything happens to me, this becomes *your* mission. Understand?"

"Yes, Captain."

"This is a matter of life and death."

The bosun, looked uneasy.

"Death, you say?"

"Yes, there are forces aboard the *Wulf* that may try to stop me."

"May I know what this is about?"

"I suppose you have a right to know. The package contains letters from princes, clients and company employees, giving evidence of alleged corruption and treason on Hartman's part. He has threatened the whole enterprise here. They don't really need us. We are here on sufferance. The Moghal Aurangzeb, Emperor of India, could drive us out with little more effort than a wave of his flywhisk. As it is, we pay a large annual sum to the princeling, the Raja of Tanjore, to have this trading post. Apparently, Hartman has upset them. Also, there is the matter of Hartman starting to build, what looks like, a fort."

The bosun looked askance: "Hartman might be a pompous braggart at worst, but there is no doubt that he is a valiant soldier, and a national hero. He's a Danish patriot. I named one of my children after him."

"Yes, that's true. But during his life, he has also fought for Germany, the French and the Venetians, too."

"Still, such accusations."

"That is why I said 'alleged'. Anyway, none of this is our concern, we must just obey orders — agreed?"

"Yes, Captain."

"I won't ask you to swear on the Bible because you are a trusted friend, as well as bosun — but I would otherwise. That's how important this is. I repeat: a matter of life and death. Understand?"

"I understand."

"It's just a precaution. You probably won't need to be involved at all. Now let's have a drink to a successful voyage home, and to seeing our wives and families."

Just then a cloud must have passed the sun, or a sail flapped loose in the breeze, as a shadow overcast the cabin skylight.

☽ ☯ ☾

Hartman sat thinking of all of the troubles and dangers he had survived, and of a possible solution to his current problem. The ship must not reach its destination. What would stop the ship? Storm: out of his control. Mutiny: too difficult to arrange. Shipwreck: too difficult to arrange and survive. Pirates: easy to arrange, with the added benefit of a split ransom and selective survival.

Hartman sent a fast cutter bearing a sealed note in code off to the south west, as he had done many times before. The note contained a ship's name and description, the date and time of its sailing and, unusually, the intimation that a friend of the recipient would be aboard.

☽ ☯ ☾

Klein was pleased that the *Flying Wulf* cast off at the tide and time of day scheduled. Free of Tranque, he was safe from any surprises or accidents that the Hartman might devise. That just left the perils of the voyage, and the presence of the unknown crew members that he suspected Hartman had infiltrated or bribed, to worry about. Ten days out, two strange craft appeared from the east. His glass revealed that they were armed and moving too swiftly to be traders. Having ordered the helmsman to turn from them and increase their speed, a stern chase developed. Klein intended to make use of his long-barrelled stern chaser guns as he'd noticed that their pursuers had no forwarding cannon. Either they chased him under his bombardment, or they turned to use their broadside and fell behind. On his orders, his guns were fired. This is when Hartman intervened.

"I have fought at sea many times. My career and my reputation is built on it. So listen to my advice. This is not the right approach. Turn and fight them — Danes don't run. Board them!"

"We will proceed as I have ordered. My first duty is to get the ship home. We can outrun them."

"You may be Captain, but as a high official of the company, senior to you in every way, I must overrule your decision."

"I refuse. You hear that helmsman — you only take orders from me."

"Yes, Sir."

He had known the helmsman, Hans, since he was a youth — no problem there.

Hartman snorted and stormed off to towards the guns. "I'll make use of my experience elsewhere then."

At the stern, Klein noticed that Hartman seem to be acquainted with the gunner. He also noticed that all of the shots fired so far had been well off target. Anyone could miss on a lifting and falling ship, but the timing and placement were wrong. The gunner was observing the shots but correcting in the wrong direction if one came close. Klein was about to takeover on the other gun when a shot from it brought down the foremast of the closest craft. It slewed round colliding violently with the other pursuer. Entangled and slowing, the pirates were left far behind. Klein, who had just reached the stern, was troubled to see Hartman's face register shock rather than surprise, and, had he imagined it, dismay rather than delight?

☽ ✪ ☾

Trouble followed trouble. Hartman had been generous to the crew with his private supply of provender. He was always scrupulous to ask the Captain's permission first though. Klein could hardly refuse without appearing ungracious and mean-spirited. Anyway, they had sufficient basic rations, so was it not better to use the more perishable luxuries early on the voyage whilst they were good?

All on board were subject to the full blast of Hartman's charm, charisma and storytelling. He had sung a very funny and obscene song about the Raja of Tanjore. His anecdotes were thrilling and comical, and his bravery modestly understated. He was always inclusive of his audience: "If you had been there, you would have enjoyed it, lads!" At other times, he would look doleful. Yet, with professions of loyalty to the King and Company, he would elicit sympathy for his circumstances, which, in the confines of a ship, were common knowledge by now. The bold, national hero traduced by lesser men — such an injustice. Suspicion and rumour spread throughout the ship from the bilges to the fighting tops.

By the time they'd reached the South Atlantic, loyalties were formed. The crew had, as far as the allocation of duties allowed, subtly shifted into two groups, those for Klein and those for Hartman. Even the mess arrangements reflected this. Suspiciously, instances of food poisoning chiefly ailed Klein's faction, with worryingly high mortality rates.

With each foreign port they called into for water, Klein lost a few more crew members; the majority being those he knew and trusted. There was little else Klein could do but keep his men busy. He had to: with the food-poisoning outbreak, and the usual accidents, the ship was rapidly becoming undermanned.

With the increased workload came resentment. The officers on board refused to step in and lend a hand as it was considered "bad for discipline." The frigate was not up to the standard demanded of a Company ship; it was drab, dirty, loose and cluttered. Neither the officers nor the crew were satisfied. Bickering and blows were exchanged in the passing, and friction of deck-life which inevitably came to a head. A fight erupted between the bosun and a topsman over an ignored order. A sharp reproach and a sullen bared-teeth response, accompanied the swing of a fist. Klein had been expecting this and yanked the topsman back by his queued hair.

"Put this man in chains now! I'll deal with him later. Back to your work!"

Hartman's guttural voice interrupted, "Hold on! I saw it all. The bosun struck first. This man is deaf in one ear from gunnery. It is an injustice. Something I know much of…"

Klein, now red with anger, could not afford to risk his authority:

"I am the Captain here, Sir! Do not dare to countermand my orders on my own deck! Put this man in chains, I say!"

Several pairs of eyes looked from Hartman to Klein, and back again.

"Leave him!"

"Either he goes in chains or you do," was Klein's retort.

"Take him," commanded Hartman.

With this final command, men pushed forward and a canvas bucket was thrust over Klein's head and his arms were pinioned. It was at this moment that Klein realised the fight between the bosun and topsman had been staged. His muffled cries, "Captain… laws of the sea…" turned the incident to a farce.

꒒ ꙮ ꒰

Hartman started to wonder whether he'd gone too far with talk of a trial. Criticisms were voiced by the officers. "He is the Captain." "You say he has been arrested… on what charges?" and most telling of all: "If, as rumour has it, you are going to be trialled in Copenhagen, why shouldn't he?"

But Hartman had thought all this through beforehand. He was a soldier, as well as a seaman: the attack, defence, and counter-attack pattern of warfare had prepared him for all exigencies.

"We are all officers of the Danish East India Company: you, me, the Captain. My rank exceeds that of the Captain. I would remind you of the Company law regarding precedence at sea between Company-officers and captains, which I am sure that you all remember from your training."

Hartman paused to let the officers ponder this obscure and invented legality before continuing:

"I accuse Captain Klein of insubordination. That is the charge. As regards to waiting until we return to Denmark, any legal action against me merely concerns an enquiry about technical matters — I have not been arrested. More importantly, those matters do not risk the safety of the ship. I am aware that Captain Klein has brought quite a few of his personal friends and shipmates into this crew. That is why the Captain must be tried now, and the matter settled before sides are taken and we have a mutiny on our hands. Do any officers disagree?"

No-one demurred. By now the gun locker had been opened and weapons were in the hands of those men loyal to Hartman.

The trial was by the book, and as short as the book was long.

Only Hartman and the ship's officers were present.

The "facts" were recounted and, by a majority, Klein was found guilty.

The following day, gagged and hooded, he was led onto the deck. After a brief announcement of the charge and sentence, Klein was hauled up to a yard-arm. He was left there for two bells, swinging to the bucking of the ship in a lively sea. Klein's adherents were shocked and intimidated.

The bosun, sequestered below, was questioned privately for several days. He must have resisted as, when he was dragged up from below, he could barely talk through his smashed teeth. He was a broken man. Hartman, with an air of clemency, ordered a dozen lashes. Even worse, he stripped the bosun of his rank, leaving him to the mercy of the crew. From then on, he was like a wounded animal, hunted in the darkness below and jostled and bullied in his unpleasant and dangerous deck-duties. Before the flogging was executed, strangely, Hartman relented due to the ex-bosun's ill health and state of mind. Every last dissenter understood the message when he disappeared one evening. The following Sunday's sermon touched on the sin of suicide.

Sitting with the cargo manifest, Hartman now knew where the letters were — the evidence of his ill-doings. Hidden under tons of cargo, the letters were completely inaccessible whilst they were at sea. Clever old Klein. Bosun Paulsen's revelations under duress may not be totally reliable though. There was a chance he had lied about the precise location of the letters. However, the bosun had revealed the letter of authority Klein had given him to gain fast access to the most senior Company members. Hartman knew that Klein would have been smart enough to send similar letters, to inform the Directors of the secret of the ship's cargo, through other means, assuming concealment of the letters had not been pre-arranged. On his arrival in Denmark, he would be arrested, or at least suspended as a prelude, before the ship was unloaded. He, Hartman, was sunk — or he would be if the ship reached Denmark.

He had to eradicate those letters. The only sure way was to destroy the ship itself.

A storm in the mid-Atlantic forged a common purpose and distraction amongst the divided crew, but it cost them a mast and an anchor.

The majority of Hartman's chosen men were more skilled at soldiering by boarding enemy ships, rather than seamanship. As such, there were too few skilled seamen to crew the ship.

But where and how was he to sink the ship? Certainly not anywhere near Denmark. Yet, he had to be near enough to civilisation for him to return. It couldn't be off of Spain, or any Catholic or Moslem country he had spent much of his life fighting. The weather also needed to be good enough so that he could escape drowning. It would be better to damage the ship on rocks so it would actually sink, not on sand where the tide could make the outcome doubtful.

He looked at the map and asked his accomplices to share their knowledge.

"Well, not the Netherlands — all sandbanks."

"Not France, Catholic, and you've had too much action against them — and who knows what the current political situation is!"

"It's got to be England."

"We are roughly in the English Channel anyway, passing Cornwall. We want a reef or rocks the ship can't miss and easy landing nearby, for our escape."

"Here! This small island with a reef extending southward is ideal. We can hide some of the goods in the cargo out of sight of the mainland. It would be a short row ashore in our longboats."

"Then what?"

"A good few months getting home. Some letters to friend's in Denmark to prepare the way; a little gold to smooth the way. Then a national hero's return from pirates, mutiny, storms and a shipwreck."

"Storm? Look it's fine weather. There's a brisk breeze — nothing more."

A few hours later, and according to the chart, St George's Island appeared where expected, off the port quarter. At gunpoint they made the crew lower the Captain's barge and a longboat. They each loaded their own caches with valuables — gold coins, rubies, diamonds, emeralds, and jade, all wrapped in long, pocketed leather pouches — into the boats. Next, they assembled the crew between decks and locked them in. The *Flying Wulf*, towing its boats close by, sailed on towards the white water ahead.

One of Hartman's men volunteered to stay behind at the wheel, holding a gun to the helmsman's head.

When he heard the whistle from the boats alongside, he clumped the helmsman over the head with the butt of his gun, ran and climbed down into the Captain's barge. The lines were cut. Their boats leapt up and down as the large ship passed them by in full sail.

The helmsman crawled along the deck and then staggered, holding his head. He quickly released the men locked below. Relieved of the threat of violence from their fellow men they soon became aware of the threat from the looming reef. But it was too late.

Some ran for the helm, others for the ratlines to reach the fighting tops.

The onlookers in the boats — those not rowing furiously for the island — looked on in fascinated horror. A long, grinding crunch followed and the ship heeled over. However, at this point, a wave lifted it and swept it past the rocks and into clear water.

In the ship's barge, Hartman paused in his attempts to raise the small sail.

"Damn!" he said pointing at the receding *Wulf*, "it floats."

"Not for long, it's certainly holed below water, and there's a whole wide bay ahead." "I think it hit a bit of a gap, it's a shame the tide wasn't lower."

"Forget that for now — the island — watch out for rocks."

"We can get in there. See, there's a path and steps."

The *Flying Wulf* sailed on across the bay with arguments raging. A man was sent below to gauge the water in the hold. "At the rate we are filling, we won't make the sandy beach ahead. Jettison the guns!" They managed to heave two guns overboard, but it was a hopeless attempt and wasted precious time. They hadn't the manpower to jettison the deck cargo, or the cargo in the hold.

"There is a small beach, closer over to the north-east. We might make that."

The helm was turned. The large ship was sluggish and turned slowly. Then — it may have been the river current flowing from the small valley to their left — the ship seemed to shift sideways and out to sea. "We'll not make it! Try and aim for that tiny beach... to the left." The great ship's wheel was spun again and the ship turned slowly, heeling over, almost at right angles to the shore. Any hope they had of reaching the sand passed. The jutting rocks ahead were approaching fast. As one, they panicked and headed for the shrouds, racing up the masts to tie themselves fast, with knives ready to cut free.

The wiser of the men threw off their clothes to make for easier swimming. The *Flying Wulf* gouged its way into a gully, scraping and scoring its bulwarks, and slid to a heavy halt. One of the two remaining masts came crashing down across the deck. Men on the fallen mast were plunged underwater and frantically cut themselves free, hauling themselves onto the mast. Not all luck is bad. The fallen mast formed a blessed bridge to the mainland and life. Some of the lesser brave souls who were on the mizzen mast stayed there the whole day, until the tide subsided again, allowing them to climb down. By then it was early evening and a horde of locals had stormed the wreck, breaking open the crates on the deck and carrying off what they could load on sleds and barrows in a most skilful manner. Broken blue and white Chinese porcelain was strewn across the deck and rocks. The crew were not ill-treated, just pushed out of the way. Someone even pointed them towards the town, shouting at the foreigners: "Looe, go Looe!" There was more violence aimed at their Cornish neighbours from the locals than towards them — the Danes looked on, bemused. Shivering, they slipped and slid their way to the shore.

Further away on the island, but with the shipwreck and the lights that bobbed about around it in sight, Hartman and his men sat around a small fire, roasting potatoes. The sparks dancing up to reach the stars above. It was a lovely night. At a small cottage, they had exchanged a few coins for fish, bread, apples and root vegetables. Joachim was thanked and thumped on the back as a good fellow for having the foresight to bring some gin.

They discussed the events of the day. "Why have a helmsman ready at a crucial moment, then bash him on the head? Why not just tie the ship's wheel?" someone whinged.

"Oh! God! I can't think of everything. If we'd tied the wheel and one of the crew got free via a gun port or something... what then?"

"Well, hitting the bloke on the head won't look good when we get back to Copenhagen!"

"That's months — maybe a year — away. He might have been killed in the wreck over there. And as far as they will be concerned, this was in the aftermath of a mutiny."

"You hope, Sir. Things can look very different in court."

"It'll be fine. Time and distance to manoeuvre — that's the key. Allow luck some play! It's brought me through alive, rich and famous. That's Hartman's Luck remember."

He raised his stoneware mug for a refill and they all laughed and drank "to Hartman's Luck!"

The stern of the model of *The Flying Wulf* built by Bernie Doyle (by kind permission of Mark Ratcliffe and the Ratcliffe family of Looe)

Historical Note

The late Ernie Ratcliffe, a local diver, spent time searching for the ship. For much of his retirement, he was towed underwater behind his boat, looking for both the *Albemarle* and the *Flying Wulf*. He found a naval pike, white and blue Chinese porcelain shards, a mug and large timbers with holes in them from teredo shipworms.

Outside Looe Museum is a Swedish cannon that was found in Looe Bay; the *Flying Wulf* was a Swedish ship captured by the Danish. Ernie believed that the hull of the ship still lies sunk in a gully, under metres of sand, probably with much of its cargo somewhere off Sherberterry Rocks, Seaton, Cornwall.

Information about the *Flying Wulf* is available by searching on the Internet via Google. Ditto Hartman, Tranque, the Danish East Indies Company and the ship's last voyage.

A coin that I found, after a powerful storm swept sand and seaweed from the beach, is from the same period of the shipwreck. That is, it is of the right Chinese dynasty. However, although the K'ang-Hsi reign ran from 1662 to 1722 and the ship was wrecked in 1691, it is quite a wide span of time. Given it was found within a few hundred yards of the putative shipwreck, I wonder what the probability is that such a coin should be found nearby if it has no connection with the *Flying Wulf*?

The bronze top of navigational dividers, used to measure distances and radii on sea charts, were found in the same vicinity and are obviously very old. They would once have had replaceable steel or wooden arms, possibly even an arm incorporating a pen.

I have imagined Hartman's character from the adventurous things that he did. I have guessed his motives based on his actions. I stress this story is fiction and I have probably been very unfair to him. However, when he eventually returned to Denmark he was reprimanded for leaving the ship and taking so long to get back from England, but he was acquitted of the original charges that caused his recall.

Perhaps much more information exists in Danish archives, but I do not have the language, or resources, to take this further.

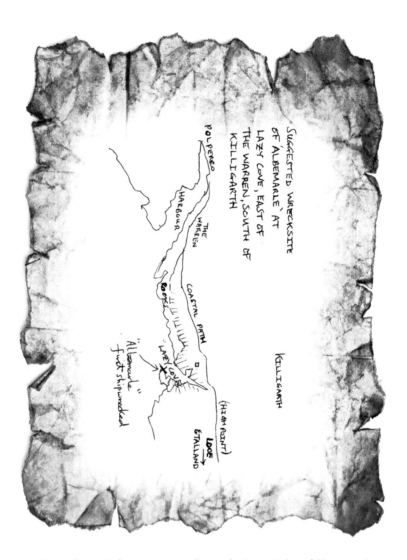

Location of the suggested wrecksite of the *Albermarle*
near Polperro

The *Albemarle,*
by the Grace of God, Ours!

1708

Captain Beawes had seen the sun-dogs on either side of the sun for several days now. It seemed as though they were chasing his ship, the *Albemarle*, the last few hundred miles home. They were bright lights in the sky, sitting either side of the sun like faithful hounds, and foretold of bad weather. He had seen many sun-dogs over his career, but these were uncommonly ominous.

His vessel belonged to the East India Company, which he had commanded for four years for a lucrative voyage trading in India, Java and the China Sea. The hold was packed with silk, indigo, jade, spices, porcelain, ivory, emeralds, and every valuable of the East that man could imagine. The cargo was well-packed, too, in order to survive the various vicissitudes that the often violent sea threw at them. The expert trading officials on board — the "supercargoes" — and their staff had wrapped, cushioned and crated the goods according to their specific perishability, fragility and vulnerability to seawater. And, of course, their value and fenceability: the gems — rubies and diamonds — that made the eyes widen and the mouth gasp, were closeted away from lustful sight like virgin nuns. Long, leather bulses, each with numerous pockets, were used to hold the gems within the darkness of locked chests; chests that were guarded day and night in the firearms room close to his cabin. Why was he musing on cargo that belonged to the Company investors — who were going to receive a huge return on their investment? Because, like the rest of his crew, he had been permitted an apportionment of space, concomitant with his status, to hold his "private trade". This was part of his pay and with it, this time, he could retire to Wales and marry a certain special female who had given her promise. A good woman, a churchgoer, who would have waited patiently through all of these, still, childbearing years. He had written to her from the ship's last port of call — Jamaica — and promised to be home by Christmas. He was determined that they would have their dream fulfilled come storm, tempest or dogs in the sun.

Away to starboard, he could see his colleague's ship, the East Indiaman "Rochester". There was no need to signal as their destination was obvious and necessary, based on the sky.

They would make Falmouth in a few hours. It was the first reasonable harbour in the English Channel where they could dock to send messages, take on water and hear of any news, such as who the country was currently at war with. It was also the last harbour that, despite the wind direction, they could sail from again, weather permitting. In his pocket, close to his heart, he could feel the comforting bulk of his next letter to Gwen. Soon it would be on its way to Wales, whilst he and his ship sailed on to London.

As they entered Carrick Roads, the large deep water harbour at the mouth of the River Fal, he left it to his sailing master to avoid the pennoned Black Rock, the deadly underwater hazard that seemed be there as a last trap for any vessel that had successfully negotiated the Manacles ledges that guarded the western approaches. Ahead was the welcome sight of several Royal Navy frigates, which would guard, his ship, and the convoy of other merchant ships he would join on the last leg of his voyage to London, recompense and landlubber respectability.

The vicar of Talland, James Cummings, was contemplating the middling spring, summer and autumn that he and his parishioners had endured. The harvest had been gathered, brought in and well-stored, but to no great volume. Similarly, the shoals of pilchards were now salted in barrels. His own small parcel of land had produced a similar proportion to that of the Lord of the Manor. On his stipend, he, like his poor parishioners, would face hungry days, unlike the Lord.

He brought his thoughts back to composing his sermon; he could provide food for their souls if not their bodies. His theme would be inspiring: hope for better times and have faith that the Good Lord will provide. And, a thought stirred in his mind, God forgive him, the hope of a local shipwreck.

Samuel Willcock of Polperro, as he thought himself to be, was reluctantly doing his figures, scratching away with a quill pen at his official account books, occasionally referring to the unofficial ones. Well, he smiled, he wasn't really of Polperro, more like he was accepted for his useful skills. He was still considered a foreigner, as one or two older locals could remember that he and his father had come to the village twenty-two years ago. Wisely, his old man had married the daughter of one of the most respected families, and he had followed suit. He was pleased to have done so as, surprisingly, despite being so cut-off from the outside world, this tiny fishing village sported a population that was taller, fitter and more intelligent than those in the surrounding counties. He supposed it had something to do with the fact that they only accepted just enough outsiders to avoid the Shibboleths of inbreeding, ensuring that those who were accepted, were tested and shared their own views of loyalty and independence. It was more preferable for them to take in those who came from further afield, rather than their own fellow Cornish. People who did not fit in with Polperro's ways were driven out. Anyone who betrayed them to the enemy — the French, the Spanish or the English authorities — were dealt with in "the old way". They disappeared: killed, gutted and weighted down; they were consigned to the depths.

He shivered and the pen nib shot spots of ink across the paper. Then he sneezed, sending various papers sailing lazily away. Not much profit this year. He needed money to invest and prosper. His dream was to provision a sleek, well-armed ship for the purpose of smuggling and privateering — licenced piracy against the Queen's enemies. The world was mad. A ship of fools. But then, wherever a fool and his money could be parted, there was Sam Willcock. That was the way of the world, too.

On the second day, after docking, the weather ameliorated. Captain Beawes and his peers were due to meet with the Royal Navy frigate commanders at the Admiral Blake Inn to discuss the convoy for the next leg of the journey to the ship's various home ports: Plymouth Portsmouth, and London. Before he entered the inn, he had just enough time to open the letter that had been delivered to his ship as he'd hurried down the gangplank, past the armed guard. He suppressed his joy at recognising the neat handwriting. Opening his clasp knife — the one that she had given him — he carefully sliced the letter open. Standing at a landing window, with folk bustling by, he read and re-read the words, hoping for a nuance or a scintilla of hope for an alternative meaning. But clearly, the lines had been crafted with school-teacherly skill to preclude all such interpretation. Although generous in praise of his character, the message was lucid: his darling had married another. Anger and sorrow churned his stomach. His throat was as constricted as the young pig he had once seen crushed by a snake. He did not notice the ring that had fallen from the letter; now lying on the floorboards. He felt a hand on his back as a fellow captain clapped him hard on the shoulder, "Come on, we're late." Beawes followed him into the crowded boisterous room, where the meeting had already started.

Discussions about the number of anchors and hawsers, the state of sails, watering and victuals went on; he was not quite oblivious to the discussion as he noticed, as if from afar — the blue mountains of Wales — that his answers were correct and cogent. He'd handed command of himself to some ghostly auto-pilot. The potential weather was discussed next. The assembled professionals vied with each other to mouth every saw, harbinger and superstition a seaman could think of. He sat in silence. Eventually, the senior in rank, acting as chairman, warned that the Royal Navy frigates had been ordered to the Downs. The merchant ships that had chosen not to accompany them on this journey would be left to either risk the attentions of the French later, or have to wait a considerable length of time for further protection. Time was money; getting to market first was vital for profit. Losing a ship was disastrous to both investors and captains. But none of those considerations touched Beawes's consciousness. When the vote to sail on the morrow came, his hand just rose upward of its own accord.

☽ ☯ ☾

At sea again, he felt he was heading nowhere. The wind and tide were favourable and a quick dash out to sea and up the Channel would see the ship in Plymouth by nightfall. But he would still be in the same place. The best he could hope for now was decades of walking a ship's deck. His officer's spirits were high as they neared home. But the dogs were still by the sun. Bright dogs by the sun, but a black dog in his heart.

The ship's routine carried on as usual but then, as though a consequence of his despair, the weather worsened. The wind picked up and the waves piled up into buffeting humps of viciousness, batting the hull from side to side and up and down, cascading the decks with white spume and water. Bending the ship over, the change of wind forced her onto a dreaded lee-shore. Charts were held down whilst courses were recalculated so they would sail into the wind, as much as the current and tide allowed, in order to clear the land downwind. By the time this was done, the factors had changed and disaster was unavoidable. Waiting for them, through the wind and curtains of rain, was a rocky anvil, upon which the storm could hammer the ship to pieces. Despite their efforts to steer the ship away from the land to port of them, the backing wind forced the bows landward with the strength of a fighter applying a headlock, determined to break an opponent's neck. An anchor was dropped, its chains clinking like falling coins. The ship groaned and creaked with the strain and the sea rushed over the gyrating bowsprit. The cable broke. The bows bucked and the ship turned, racing downwind again. Beawes ordered the iron cannons to be jettisoned, and this dangerous work was started. More effort was wasted dropping the ship's last anchor with the same result as before, although this time the cable whipped a man overboard. There would be no riding out this storm — their last hope had gone with the sound of the cable parting; their very own crack of doom.

They did not know where they were. Through the roaring gloom they could see lights twinkling to their left. The officers decided they should go with the wind and not fight it; turn onto the opposite tack and head for what might be a haven. Beawes was strangely calm and unresponsive, hanging on to the safety lines like everyone else and staring, unseeing. The officers took his single nod as an agreement and ordered the crew into action. Eventually they saw the rocks and the towering cliffs, but realised that the lights they'd been heading towards might as well have been stars, for all their hope of reaching them.

A great water-filled crevice in the rocks lay ahead of them. The white water foaming at its mouth hid its rocky jaw. This was their destination. The hull was lifted by a great breaker and deposited firmly on the rocks, like a giant's hands might place a baby in a cradle. There lay, still battered by ensuing waves, a wreck but secure. All on board held their breath, waiting for the next big wave, for the inevitable shift and capsize. But, to their relief, the tide was going out and they remained in place, hammered, but unmoving. Under the looming cliffs, the darkness gathered around them. Beawes and his officers swiftly dismissed any thought of trying for the shore. Incredibly, for the moment, this splintering, creaking wreck was the safest place to be until daylight allowed them to evaluate their situation. Each member of the crew secured themselves, above or below deck, according to their reckoning of the danger. One man even climbed a mast to a fighting top believing the theory that the mast would eventually fall towards the land and deliver him safely onshore. Most of them huddled together for warmth, and hugged themselves in fear.

It was a fisherman, up early and trudging up the hill to get some potatoes for his stew and the perchance of picking mushrooms, who first saw the *Albemarle*. He observed carefully, then dropped everything he was carrying, and ran. He'd heard that, in London, they had something called a lottery that could make a man rich for life. This was the village of Polperro's lottery. Every man in the village had a plan in their head, for what they would do if they were to suddenly become rich. Likewise, everyone in the village had rehearsed and discussed what they would do if a large shipwreck should come their way. The first questions his fellows were likely to ask would be regarding the size and type of vessel; he was ready with the answers. They all knew — men, women and children — what tools, barrows, sledges and pack-animals to take. What responsibility each had. What to salvage first. They even knew what to do with the crew — get them out of the way quickly and humanely so there were no witnesses and no recriminations. This way, the owners of the vessel could be charged for their sailor's accommodation and subsistence for longer.

It was also clear what they should not do — tell any other

village. Nor the nobility, in case they claimed it all by manorial right. The violent tinners in the mines were not to be told either — they'd have the lot.

It was common knowledge that there would be fair shares for everyone in the village. It was the best way to make sure everyone complied, and ensured self-interest and secrecy.

The *Albemarle* was theirs by the grace of God, and the capriciousness of the sea.

There, seeing all and organising all, was Willcock, whilst his calculating mind was working on ways of getting that little bit extra. It was entirely acceptable to charge for the use of his carts and donkeys, as well as safe storage. He, who had the means to convey the crew to safety, would have possession of them. He would also have links to the owners and the authorities — and their goodwill — naturally, the understanding that a man had to make a living would follow.

The ship was held precariously on a small island of rocks at the entrance to the water-filled ravine, whilst the seas boiled around it. The sailors could see the villagers gathering and preparing to bring equipment down the cliffs and along the undercliff. As always, the basest, perhaps being the idlest of them all, arrived first.

They had heard dreadful stories of the fate of shipwrecked mariners being drowned, stabbed, knocked on the head, or of fingers and ears being cut off to steal gold rings. It looked as if they were not to be spared as the barbarians, carrying knives and axes, laughed with glee at the sailors' predicament, beckoning whimsically with their hands.

Beawes thought of handing out firearms to his men. Hoping that, by firing, they would warn them off; yet the firearms would be useless in this weather. Cutlasses? They were outnumbered and swimming with a weapon in these waves would be the equivalent of choosing to drown. Forcefulness would just inflame the waiting mob.

In the Indies, he had always found that it was always better to approach natives in a peaceful manner; to be suspicious and on guard whilst smiling and appearing not to be.

Shortly, a small group of men arrived. A pistol was drawn from under an oilskin and fired in the air. An authoritative voice shouted, while his arms pointed and gesticulated purposely. The mob looked on and then parted as the newcomers advanced to the brink of the tumult. After some failed throws judged the distance and cast grappling hooks onto the *Albemarle.*

Shouts of "After, after — you'll get all!" and waving cudgels kept the rougher elements back.

The crew were surprised by the skill and care with which they were rescued from the vessel. With yelled encouragement, sailors part swam, part hauled themselves along the ropes towards the land. Some of the village men, with ropes around their waists, waded into the shallows with gaffs and hooked the sailors, dragging their catches gasping onto the rocks. Beawes was the last to leave, taking a leap into the white foam. He was dragged onto the shore unhurt. His clothes were heavy with water when a sudden wave bowled him over.

His head struck the rocks and he was knocked unconscious. He awoke, what he judged to be a short time later, to find himself laid out well above the high tide mark, the deep graze on his head stinging from the salty water.

He could hear that well respected voice still calling out and issuing orders. In response, children and old folk hurried them away from the ship. By hand, they hauled the sailors up to the coastal path, where they were put astride ponies or donkeys and led down the steep hill to the small fishing village and harbour. They were deposited in cottages, fish cellars and a few houses. Other, older, people took their soaking clothes and provided them with more humble attire. Their cuts and bruises were tended to. And, with a warm fire to sit by and hot fish stew to sip, they were grateful with relief.

Beawes was with them. The shock of the shipwreck had

broken his fugue. He noticed that all of the pack-animals that had been used to convey them to the village had swiftly departed back the way they had come. Once dry and fed, most of his uniform was returned to him. He had been last off the *Albemarle* and still held the log book in its waterproof bag, tied around his neck under his shirt. Now was the time to count how many had been lost. Unsteady as he was, he insisted on a tour of his crew in their various lodgings, and completed a roll call. He had lost seven men since leaving Falmouth: two had fallen from the yards, one killed when the cable parted, and the rest had been swept overboard. Nearly all the others had cuts, grazes and bruises. There were a few broken fingers, but overall, they had been the subject of great good luck. Then sleep overwhelmed them all.

☽ ☻ ☾

Beawes awoke weak and tired. Daylight and memory rendered him heir to all of his troubles. In the space of twenty-four hours, he had lost shipmates, his ship, his career, his wealth and Gwen. He had lost his future. Yet the thunder and sheet lightning outside the window were forcing him to stay awake and contemplate an alternative and uncharted life. That could wait, he decided. For now — there was just "now". He was safe and warm, why move?

He was suddenly disturbed by a red face peering around the door. It peered from well below the door latch height. Its appearance was followed by a squeal and the soft slap of bare feet running away. Soon after, a young woman arrived and pressed a horn beaker into his hands. He sipped: the sharp taste of hot brandy mixed with water — and some herb — warmed his throat.

He murmured his thanks as she moved to sit on the bed. Her cool fingers felt his forehead.

"I'm Captain Beawes of the East Indiaman, 'The Albemarle'".

"I know. Pleased to meet you."

"You are?"

"Mrs Willcock — Mary — Thomas Willcock's wife."

"Where am I?"

"This is Tom's study, in our house. You're in the village, Polperro, in the county of Cornwall."

"How long have I —"

"You've been asleep since ten, yesterday morning. It's now noon."

"The rest of my uniform?"

"Being dried out. We put thee abed, you's exhausted, me old handsome. We kept your book safe — we had trouble prising it from your fingers!" She gestured and he saw the ship's log safely placed on a table. Perhaps it would have been better if he'd lost it, he thought — duty runs deep. He lifted himself and realised that he was naked under some kind of nightshirt.

"It's open!" he said, indicating the log book.

"Well, we had to make sure your things were dry."

Just as he was thinking that she was a very good-looking woman, he stretched his leg and accidentally made contact. She blushed and stood up.

"Feeling better then?" she asked archly.

He sipped from the beaker and coughed.

"I'm sorry, I don't drink spirits. May I have some plain water, please?"

"You won't be wanting our water — it's tainted, from the mines up on moors. You stick with the French — good stuff that."

"But —"

"Expensive, too. There's water in it," she said seriously, as an afterthought.

"Where is your husband, if you don't mind my asking?"

"He's arranging, informing and ordering. He'll see you soon — why, he's even given you our best bed."

He looked past her and spotted his uniform jacket hanging on the back of a chair.

"My uniform — the epaulettes? And where is my watch, it was in with the log?"

"You're a poor shipwrecked sailor, battered by waves and rock. You can't expect not to suffer some wear, tear and loss. I'm sure those nice folk in London will pay you back."

"I'm very grateful but —"

"You were lucky you were wrecked amongst God-fearing Christians. Those Scillonians would have cut your throat like they did to that Admiral Cloudy ... Spade was it?"

"Cloudesley-Shovell."

"That's him. Last winter it was. No buts now. Drink-up and warm yourself inside, as well as out," she smiled, tilting the base of the horn beaker so that the fiery liquid ran down his throat, causing him to cough and splutter — tears came to his eyes.

"There, there…" she soothed, gathering his head to her breast. "You've had misfortune upon misfortune, but you mustn't be a winnard and give up!"

"What the…"

"We saved the letter, as well as the book thing," she pointed to a desk in the far corner.

There lay Gwen's letter with the envelope next to it.

"You read it!"

"Of course. You might have died. You were exhausted, cut and bruised, shivering an' all."

Died? Rubbish! Palpable nonsense! He felt his face burning from blushing.

Among the ledgers on the desk, he recognised one that was familiar.

"That one on top!" he pointed. "It's the cargo manifest."

"Yes, we saved that, too."

"That should be with Johnson, the Deputy Supercargo."

"The soupcargo? What's that?"

"A supercargo is a company agent. We've several. They each do different kinds of trading in the countries we go to."

"Anyway, he must be that little bald man who drowned trying to get that heavy tome there off the ship. I thought it was a Bible."

Poor Johnson, their supercargo — he remembered the

previous night's roll call. He glanced from log to letter to manifest: they knew all of his and the *Albemarle's* secrets. He felt naked under the blanket, and her knowing, but kindly, gaze.

☽ ☯ ☾

Willcock was tired, but elated. He hummed "Lillibulero" to himself, faster and faster as he hurried to a late breakfast with his guest.

"Captain Beawes, how happy I am to see you looking so well."

Beawes took the proffered hand and shook it uncertainly, his gathering complaints slack on his tongue.

"Is the ship lost?"

"By no means, it is still perched like a ravished mermaid on a rock."

"I must see the ship."

"Oh! not possible at the moment I'm afraid. Our brave villagers are defending it, fighting off the foreigners."

"Who?"

"Foreigners: tinners, men from other villages, Looe, Pelynt and Talland."

"What are tinners or did you say sinners?"

"No, tinners it was — miners for tin. Hard, drunken, violent men, armed with shovels and picks."

"They're here?"

"No — but they will be soon. At any moment. We have men out in the lanes watching for them."

"I must contact the authorities."

Willcock looked blank for a moment.

Beawes persevered: "The local Squire, the JP, the owners in London, the insurers, and my employers, the East India Company."

"All in hand. I had a look in your log and spoke to your officers."

"That was for me to do!"

"In your state, with your troubles —"

"But…"

"You drink up now."

"Is there no damned water?"

"Can't have you poisoned, I've a responsibility to your employers."

☽ ☉ ☾

Beawes insisted on writing a letter to Mr Wooley at East India House in London. Despite sealing it, he was somehow sure that Willcock would read it, so he mentioned the gentleman's efforts to rescue the crew and the accommodation provided. Other than the basic facts, there was little else he could tell his masters regarding the present condition and location of the *Albemarle*, and the safety of the cargo.

As the days passed and the brandy dulled his critical faculties, Beawes was content with deferring his date with the wreck, and the reckoning with his employers. His officers visited, with not much to report. The Chief Supercargo, Joseph Bullock, expressed his frustration at not being able to get to the shipwreck. He even admitted that he was not actually aware of its exact position, as his travel from the shore to the village had been erratic in the early morning gloom. Beawes realised that he was similarly in the dark as he had little memory of his journey to the village. His crew seemed happy to await events, grateful to the villagers for their survival. They spent their time making friends, helping out, playing with the children, forming liaisons with the local maidens, and spinning stories of their travels and the mysteries of the Orient. They received much encouragement. A great favourite were the two pet monkeys — which were still terrified and being coaxed — that had been rescued from the ship.

Tom and William, as they now addressed one another, spent the winter evenings smoking uncommonly good tobacco. He heard Willcock tell of his early life in Somerset, and of him seeing, aged ten years, the Duke of Monmouth. "No further away than from here to the far quay," he said, pointing across the windswept harbour with his pipe stem. Memories of the

1685 Monmouth Rebellion and Willcock senior's foolish decision to join the losing side followed, along with an account of his father's heroic efforts to save him after the Battle of Sedgemoor. How they fled as fugitives, hunted from county to county by dragoons, hearing firstly of rebels being strung up to trees and inn signs, and later of Judge Jefferies and the Bloody Assizes. Cold, hunger and the constant threat of betrayal left them little choice but to live in the wind-stricken woods and on the moors, whilst the market squares of west country towns stank from the stench of the steaming offal of hanging, drawing and quartering — the Traitor's Death.

They always headed towards the sunset. One day, on foot, horses long sold, they heard hooves behind them. In practised alarm, they darted from the track they were on to another, more verdant, path that promised concealment. This chance turn led them to Polperro and the sea.

There was a pause in this odyssey as pipes were refilled, tamped and relit, during which Beawes realised that these disclosures, that had once been considered treason, were no longer compromising to Willcock. Since then, William of Orange had invaded and displaced the previous King James in the bloodless revolution of 1688. William died and now his sister-in-law, Queen Anne, was on the throne.

Nevertheless, each seeming confidence engendered reciprocal disclosures, empathy and good fellowship.

Willcock was a self-made man like Beawes — ambitious for himself and his family, but honourable in his own way. What, thought Beawes, had his own honour and duty done for him? It was who you gifted or sold these things to that mattered. By the time Willcock had asked him to sign receipts and letters, Beawes knew, and accepted, the situation; he was complicit. What was there to go back to anyway? Just as Willcock and his father had relinquished their Somerset life, Beawes had given up his past life in Wales, The East India Company and the Indies.

His praise of the evening's French brandy and best Virginia tobacco gave Willcock the opportunity to explain the local economy to him.

"Fishing, and what little vegetables we grow on the undercliffs, feed us — no-one starves. But for a better life, free trade and privateering are Polperro's mainstay."

"So breaking the law: smuggling and piracy, and stealing from wrecked ships!" Beawes was amazed by his own audacious conclusion. However, it seemed appropriate as Mrs Willcock arrived with two cups of coffee, which he was fairly sure had come from the *Albemarle's* cargo. It was an expensive beverage for a small fishing village.

As Willcock lifted his cup and sniffed the aroma there was a glint of humour in his eyes, rather than hostility.

"A little harsh, perhaps. When in Rome? Cornwall is a different country from England, and Polperro is a different country from Cornwall."

"How so?"

"We depend on no-one. So why pay tax? What for? We use the sea. We defend ourselves. We feed ourselves. We owe no loyalty, except to one another."

There was a long silence whilst Beawes considered this.

He had never drunk brandy before the shipwreck. He had believed in God and the Bible, until he'd read that letter at Falmouth. He had believed in the King, and duty, too. So many of his beliefs had been wrecked by the recent events.

Willcock broke into his reverie: "Relax, you're safe. We speak our minds here."

"But my ship is being looted."

"Your ship is beyond the reach of those in London. It might as well be lost in the China Sea."

"They'll send searchers, armed men, offer rewards, and bring the local law down on you."

"We're hardly on the map; no roads either. They'll have trouble finding Polperro. They'll only find the *Albemarle* when we are ready for them to find it."

For a moment, Beawes felt uneasy with the possessive manner by which Willcock spoke of his ship — it wasn't a complete wreck yet.

Willcock anticipated him: "Look out of the window. This is one of the worst storms of this, or the last, century. It won't abate before the tides spring. The ship's done for if it stays where it is. Same if it washes away."

Beawes nodded. He had worked this out hours ago.

"But they'll come."

"Not by sea in this weather. Besides, it's invisible from land, except from one point on the coastal path. Even if they do come, no-one will give them shelter here, or sell them food."

"If not the authorities, men from other villages and these tinners?"

"Oh, we've dealt with them before. Same applies: they don't know the exact location. That's been our secret for a very — little — lucrative while."

"They'll find it."

"We'll fight them off in the hollow lanes and block access to the village."

They savoured their coffee as they both considered the matter. Beawes changed the subject somewhat: "You said that Cornwall — Polperro — is a different country from England, yet no-one speaks Cornish — as I've heard a few still do in the far west?"

"No. In Queen Elizabeth's time they did, but luckily for me, by 1686 it had died out. They only remember a few basic words and these are taught to the children."

"Like what?"

"Oh, counting up to ten. Colours, animal and flower names. Sentiment, I suppose."

"What's a 'winnard'?"

"A weakling — my wife calls me that when I moan about a head cold."

"You smiled earlier when I mentioned the law?"

"Well, I smiled because you said 'local law'. We can deal with that alright. We know the local squires and burgesses. We can hire lawyers. We form the juries."

"The laws of the land? Parliament?"

"It is rare for a Cornish jury to find a smuggler guilty. And London? They can't ride roughshod over Cornish customs and rights. In 1688 a Cornish army marched on London over some religious disagreement. It was when the old King sent old Bishop Trelawney and other bishops to the Tower."

"They were massacred, as I remember."

"True. Stupid lot of farm-boys mainly. Very sad… following preachers and their betters, and not thinking for themselves."

"Proves my point."

"Not really. Along with Sedgemoor, it helped bring the old King down."

"That was for religious reasons — they all thought he was a papist."

"They won't want trouble in Cornwall because such things lead to the French or Spanish taking advantage. They'd invade Polperro to divert troops from the continental wars."

"My God! If Polperro is a country of its own, then you must be its Minister of Foreign Affairs."

"Thank you. I like to keep myself informed. My father was a minister of the church. Thanks to him, I can read, write and figure. I've also been known to play chess with Squire Trelawney."

"The Bishop?"

"No, his brother, Sir Charles."

"And you're friendly with him?"

"That would be barred by the difference in rank. I'm useful to him, and sometimes, with all due deference and informally, I play him at chess. I let him win, of course — eventually — which in itself is quite difficult."

"He'll hardly stand by you in the matter of my ship."

"He's not often here. He'll be more concerned about getting his share, than with the law of customs."

"His share? What's he done to deserve that?"

"By ancient manorial right, the squire owns jetsam and flotsam on the shores of his manor."

"May I see my ship, please?"

"Tomorrow, we'll go tomorrow."

The next morning, Beawes drank from the village pump, suffered no ill effects and no-one said a word.

"Tainted water from the mines?" he queried. "Comes an' goes," was their response.

Although, from then on, he got fresh water whenever he requested it. A small victory.

Beawes stood on a high point on the coastal path with the clouds racing by, seemingly skimming his head. Squalls, like the wraiths of invisible ships, charged across the sea from the south west, as the wind lashed his face with cold stinging rain. The telescope that Willcock had handed him was of little use, although familiar in appearance.

Far below, the *Albemarle* squatted on the rocks like a maiden aunt caught on the privy. Her sails had been ripped and lay streaming around her bulwarks. Broken spars and hanging rigging danced back and forth. Even so, there was a lull in the stormy weather.

Cables had been rigged to secure the ship to the shore — based on their uniforms, he could tell that this was the work of his officers and men. Small boats dotted the water between the ship and the shore, sheltered from the waves by the ship. Still, he marvelled at the nerve and the skill of the oarsmen. The Polperro folk were busy with a derrick, swinging the remaining cannon ashore. Lines of other villagers, under the direction of his supercargoes, queued to collect landed cargo. Another line wended away carrying the goods, heading along the rocks towards the village. Even from his vantage point, he could see that little of the cargo was reaching the path to Polperro. Much was being hidden in the undergrowth or diverted towards the rocks at the harbour entrance, where they were loaded onto small boats to be rowed across, going to who knows where. Some were coming up the coastal path towards him, then heading northwards over the hill. A small boat appeared from behind the ship. As it spun around the stern, bundles were flung into waiting hands on the rocks. Every approach to the vessel, dangerous or not, was being used by wreckers, officers, crew and officials, working alongside, but apparently ignorant of one another. The gale was an impediment to speech.

Leaning close and shouting, Beawes pointed: "Where's the deck cargo?"

"Must have been washed off. The force of the sea is a wonder."

Beawes focussed the telescope on the villagers nearest to him. They were carrying sails, ropes, hawsers, rigging, marlin spikes, cooking utensils, navigational instruments, and the binnacle. Basically, every fixture of brass or bronze was being 'unfixed' and carried away.

"I see no-one's interested in the figurehead," Beawes said dryly.

"Difficult to get to in this sea. Also, not something easily explained away... Oh! I see, you're joking."

"It's hard not to get into the spirit of things."

"Well, you've seen her now. Let's go back. Lots to do. Lots of foreigners about to arrive, I've heard."

"What? The other villages, the tinners?"

"Well, so far we've seen off Vicar Cumming of Llansallos and his small mob — we gave them some cudgel and then some cargo. With the tinners, we used brute force: no point in giving them anything, they're too greedy. They would only come back for more."

"Who then? Who's coming?"

"More official-like people. And some armed marines from Plymouth."

"Well that's it then — your game is over."

"No, we can manage it. But now it's a race against time."

In the days that followed, the weather abated and the unloading and dismantling of the ship became more fervent. A small fishing boat was able to sail back and forth between the wreck and Polperro. More derricks appeared on the shore and a stream of sledges, barrows and pack-ponies brought the cargo further inland. Crates and bundles swung wildly across the waves before a long or short pause, followed by a finely directed lowering into a waiting boat. He saw an injured man carried from the hold. Another man forgot to let go of the cargo net he was loading and was carried, hanging from it, to the shore.

Willcock casually questioned Beawes about the cargo.

"I've seen the manifest, it was with the log, but that doesn't tell me the order in which the different goods are stored, sort of top to bottom of the hold or fore and aft."

"We had some well-packed porcelain on deck. Coffee is topside as one of our last trading posts was Brazil. Sugar is from the West Indies, it has to be part of the cargo by law."

"I thought you went to the East Indies?"

"We did; it was a four year voyage. This was on the way back."

"What about the diamonds?"

"Ah! You know?"

"Of course, they're in the manifest."

"You can't take those. All hell will break loose."

"I quite agree, but that lot down there won't. But then, they don't know where they are."

Willcock suddenly stared hard at the shore.

"What the hell is that! I've never seen such a weird sea surface except when the pilchard shoals come."

"That'll be the indigo — a dye. Those bales floating on the sea have been breached and are now ruined."

"Damn! Even worse, they'll mark the sea down current and give away the wreck's position."

A slick of brilliant blue spread steadily across the waves.

Various strangers appeared in the villages, markets and towns around, making enquiries, paying for information and often just listening to the talk around them. A new phrase had entered the local dialect: "Lazy Cove". Apparently the phrase had originated from the overheard conversations between Polperro people, when they were at the market selling or exchanging their sudden wealth in goods: coffee, tea, sugar, calico, and spices. Older folk were quizzed and charts were consulted. No-one had heard of the place, not even the locals. It was a mystery. One that caused merriment at Polperro when talk of this mystery — their mystery — reached them. As Willcock explained to Beawes, "The wreck site has no name. So we made up a name for it. We're using a bit of old Cornish to confound others. It's not 'Lazy Cove', although it may sound like it to foreigners. It's actually 'Glazy Cove'. Glazy is the old Cornish for blue or bluey. We're calling it that because of the blue indigo staining the sea around there. They'll not find it on any map."

☽ ☺ ☾

The secret of the wreck site was out. A local Justice of the Peace and Trelawney's steward were on the coastal path viewing the *Albemarle* when Willcock arrived.

"A wild morning, Sirs," he greeted them amicably, as though they'd been invited.

Trelawney's man pointed down at the wreck with his riding crop, "I can see that your lads have had their sport, but I claim this wreck by manorial right for Sir Charles Trelawney, the owners — and the King." Mention of the King usually impressed simple folk, although Willcock was by no means in that category.

"Of course. Our boats, carts and ponies are at your command — for hire at very reasonable terms."

"If anyone takes goods from her that'll be theft. I don't want to have to hang anyone, so see word gets about," the JP butted in.

"Well she's all yours," Willcock said, gesturing at the

sequestered hull, surrounded by a boiling sea, that clearly held no imminent promise.

The Steward grunted, held onto his tricorne hat and wig with one hand, and turned his horse away.

☽ ☯ ☾

Half a dozen red-coated armed marines marched into the village. Here, their sergeant loudly announced that he and his men were there to guard the ship, *Albemarle*, recently wrecked hereabouts.

He was completely ignored. Lodgings and food and drink were mostly refused and instances when they did accept, made them ill or drunk. They were offered a smelly cave some distance away and the stormy weather returned. Their questions regarding the location of the ship were ignored or answered in an unintelligible dialect. When they formed separate search groups, they were harassed and misdirected. If they stayed together, their equipment was purloined and small accidents occurred. When they became aggressive an armed mob formed in response. On one occasion when they tried to search along the coastal path, they met a picket and a small skirmish ensued, during which a small cannon was fired at them. One night, they sat around a fire and, unexpectedly, a package was catapulted onto the flames. The gunpowder therein took their eyebrows off and threw them onto their backs, their arms and legs waggling like the lobsters they had been nicknamed after. Not before long, they became very jumpy and less concerned with their mission. Soon after, they formed up and marched away to Fowey, without even having seen the ship.

It was just before Christmas when a whole band of officials arrived. They were appointed by the East India Company, all with grand titles, and bearing their letters of authority: Commissioner Wright of Plymouth Dockyard; Mr Ustick, Surveyor of Plymouth; John Addis, a trusted merchant of Plymouth; Robert Bullock, an attorney from Bodmin; Mr Savage, Secretary of Customs;

Captain Sandys, a Naval officer — all cordially welcomed by Thomas Willcock and Captain Beawes.

"Still here, Captain Beawes? I'm surprised that you are not on your way to London to report. Your letters are considered very light on detail, I'm told."

Willcock quickly responded: "The captain has been my guest as he was considerably battered during his escape from the wreck, last to leave of course."

"And I have a duty to the *Albemarle*, still," Beawes added.

"Well let's see the ship now!"

"Refreshments first, surely, gentlemen."

Captain Sandys was wordlessly overruled by the surge of his companions following Willcock to the kitchen, where a curtseying Mrs Willcock was cutting ham, surrounded by a mouth-watering array of food and drink.

Crew, and supercargoes joined as the officials started the long trek to the ship across the rocks. A few falls and stumbles caused considerable cursing and torn breeches but finally, the ship came into view. The mastless *Albemarle*, still with its bowsprit pointing inland, looked more like a dying elephant than a graceful seagoing vessel.

Captain Sandys stripped off his uniform jacket, hat and sword and insisted on going aboard, which was achieved, albeit with difficulty, with the help of a small boat.

After an hour of boredom for the onlookers, Sandys swung himself into the pitching boat. Following a few yards of skilful rowing by a local oarsman, he was able to leap adroitly ashore.

"The hull is sound; she can probably be re-floated. It's even possible that the steering hasn't been damaged."

"Incredible!" Mr Ustick gasped.

"She'll need some pumpwork, and plugging of holes with tarred sails or collision mats."

"What about the cargo — what's been saved — or stolen?" Addis enquired, glancing at the gathering village onlookers above them on the coastal path.

"I have good news," Willcock smiled.

Back in Polperro, Willcock led the way to a fish cellar at the back of his house and unlocked the double doors. Lanterns were called for and Addis and Ustick entered the dark space to find large bales and crates. They were left to delve, count and discuss the cargo manifest with the supercargoes.

In Willcock's kitchen, the others huddled around the blazing fire, awaiting Addis and Ustick's return.

"Is that all there is?"

"Well, rescuing the crew was my priority. In the circumstances, in such stormy weather, you can only imagine the trouble I and my lads had getting those bulky, wet, heavy things off the ship," Willcock scorned their ingratitude.

"But…"

"All the while fighting off tinners, gypsies, and the men from Talland and Llansallos!"

"Yes, yes, I'm sure that you did your best, but the professional people are here now," Sandys irritably mollified the group.

"Well, I would point out that I am not Polperro born, hence my… er… more conventional attitude to law and order."

"Of course, Mr Ustick intended no offence," Sandys stated firmly, although Ustick gritted his teeth and stared at the ceiling.

The officials retired to another room, then returned within the hour with their decision.

Commissioner Wright, his periwig askew, acted as their spokesman.

"We'll take over from this point onwards. I have men from Plymouth, skilled at salvage, on their way to Looe. They are expected to arrive here just after Christmas to deal with the remaining cargo on board. Captain Sandys will deal with the ship."

And with that they were gone, their horses slipping and stumbling on the stony track out of the village.

Willcock sat in the Jolly Sailor Inn playing "Lillibulero" on a fife. The shrill notes of the jaunty, Jacobite song was a suitable accompaniment to the howling wind rattling the crude leaded windowpanes. Hands moved leather beer tankards and feet tapped to the music as Willcock skilfully changed the tune to "Bonnie Dundee". He then took a break to literally wet his whistle. Beawes, to see if his guess was right, took the opportunity to ask him from whence his playing ability came.

"Monmouth, 1685. As a young lad, I was taught at the campfire by Cornelius, a soldier. I snatched this fife from his dead body as we escaped. I must have been a fast learner as the rebellion was over in a month.'

Soon, all of those attending the village meeting had arrived.

Beawes had the opportunity to observe how Willcock worked his influence on the villagers. A mutiny was brewing, tempers were high — the precious ship had been discovered. They feared the cargo would be taken from them and there was talk in Plymouth of more armed men being deployed to secure the ship until it, or its cargo, could be taken beyond their reach.

"Over my dead body. We'll fight 'em to the death. I'll cut the hawsers and tow her off so she sinks offshore rather than let 'em have it," the ringleader, Oliver, hissed.

With almost Socratic argument, Willcock guided the discussion, each time interjecting with: "And what happens then?" This strategy led them to the voicing of the inevitably disastrous consequences of their impassioned plans — usually the gibbet, jail or transportation to the American colonies.

Irked by the gentle despatch of all of their schemes, Oliver paused, scowled and waved an index finger at Beawes.

"What's he doing here?"

"He's my guest, and my friend," he said, to Beawes's surprise.

"Friend? Friend!"

"Yes, anyone who puts me before religion, politics, and the law, is my friend. Isn't that what holds us all together in Polperro?"

Willcock looked at Beawes apologetically, but Beawes got

the hint.

"I must go and check on my men," he stated, although he'd noticed several familiar faces amongst the fishermen.

When Beawes had gone, Oliver gathered his thoughts, twisting his baccy pipe back and forth, and continued calmly.

"Well, what should we do then?"

"How about a slight change of course, using your idea?"

"Which is?"

"Our strength is our boats, and the knowledge of the currents and rocks around here. We can cut the hawsers securing her and then move her."

"Not in this sea and these weather conditions. She won't be going anywhere, except down."

"Quite agree. If she's not moved the sea will get her soon enough, and likely sink her in deepwater. But meanwhile the law, and Navy, will get involved and we'll be done for. Do you want soldiers present in the village? — lots of them — they'll discover all your hiding places. You also run the risk of losing what you have gathered. Not to mention they could unearth your French trade, too?"

Willcock paused as the crowd considered this outlook mournfully, then continued,

"That ship is our bounty, and our doom. We need another week or two with it. Yet whilst she's here, and the law knows of her, it'll bring nothing but trouble down on us… do you see?"

"So how can we move her, and where to?"

"Is it even possible?" someone interrupted, receiving a silencing stare from both Oliver and Willcock in return. The latter answered none the less, counting off points on his fingers:

"The Royal Navy think it can be done. The hull is sound. Even if there are a few sprung boards, or even a hole, it's nothing that pumping and a cradle of plugging material in tarred sail slung underneath won't remedy. The sea's water pressure will do the rest. My man, Jenkins, was in the Navy and he's seen it done 'afore. You've all done it before, too, only on smaller vessels — remember when the Jane went aground three winters back. And we don't need it afloat for long."

"Surely it's stuck there though?"

"No, it's held there by hawsers and the low neap tide. Now, with the tide springing, it's already started to move a little underfoot at high tide. The hawsers have to be tightened every day."

"But…"

"As the spring tide flows — the same tide that put it there — we have a good chance."

"Then what? Is the steering working?"

"We won't know 'til we know."

"So, what's next?"

"We wait for a lull in the weather, then move it at night."

"Where to?"

"That's the problem. Somewhere that's closer in, more secure, and invisible from sea and land. You tell me where! You're the ones who keep telling me that your families have lived here since Noah, and know every rock, cove and current."

Oliver's mouth moved from side to side in exasperation, even though he had no pipe between his lips.

"A lull… in the weather, you say… there's no sign o' that and the law'll be here soon."

"That's the gamble we have to take — we could lose it all. We have four days before the salvagers arrive."

☽ � ☾

Willcock found Beawes in oilskins, where he guessed he would be, looking down at the *Albemarle* lathered by the raging sea. Nothing would be salvaged today. "Completely inaccessible," Beawes shouted.

On the way back to the village, Willcock led him off the coastal path and through a gate to a small planted area. Approaching a driftwood hut, he put his shoulder to the door. With the door shut behind them, and with a window formed of some sort of semi-transparent membrane, they were sheltered enough to talk freely. Boxes served as seats and Willcock drew a hipflask from his pocket, which was soon passing back and forth between them.

"I presume that the ship and cargo were insured."

"Yes."

"How so? The cargo would not be known until the return trip?"

"Insurance agents in the Indies ports — east and west."

"What about your own investment, your own private trade?"

"My 'indulgence' they call it, part of my remuneration. How do you know of that?"

"Oh, talk with your fellow officers. Was it also insured?"

"Sadly, no. Although, I may get some small compensation from the company."

"That's a cruel blow. I suppose you couldn't get it off of the *Albemarle* with that storm."

"No, it was a sea-chest that I secretly stored in forward hold A. No hope of reclaiming it now."

"What did you buy?"

"Presents for... jade, carved ivory pieces, pearls, and quite a lot of cheap diamonds. Things that did not take much space and represented — for my purse — high value."

"What will happen after this?"

"There'll be an enquiry — accusations and suspicions will be aired. They'll say I was too far back in Falmouth harbour to make a dash to sea before the weather broke. Or that I should have taken on more anchors. Eventually, I may get another ship. Not with the East India Company, though. It was a rich ship — they'll be looking for a scapegoat."

"A merchantman, though?"

"Nothing so prestigious — a coastal collier more like."

"A profession ashore then?"

"I've been at sea all of my life. To move to land, I'd need money to buy an inn or ships' chandlers."

"Wales?"

"Nothing to go back for."

"Look, I hope to have a ship built — a three-masted lugger,

for use as a privateer, as well as free trade. With the goodwill of Squire Trelawney, I should be able to get letters of marque to attack the King's enemies at sea — a changing, but always numerous target. I'll need a master for it."

"You mean me?"

"Why not? You've sailed long voyages, fought off pirates and natives. You've knowledge of ordnance and navigation, and commanded men."

"Me? After the *Albemarle* wreck. My lack of judgement they'll conclude."

"It's me you're talking to, not 'them'. No-one could have sailed the *Albemarle* to safety in that storm. Many ships were wrecked. Even Royal Navy frigates, much more seaworthy than merchantmen, foundered."

"But…"

"Perhaps you were — preoccupied — but I've talked to your men. You did nothing wrong. I offer you a future, if you want it."

"I have no money to invest in your venture."

"You'd be salaried. You could choose your own crew. Have prize money. Who knows, you may even have a windfall to invest?"

"My pay will be delayed, I'm sure. And subject to many deductions."

☽ ☉ ☾

The storms continued throughout most of December. Christmas came and passed. On the first day of the New Year, 1709, the wind lessened. Captain Beawes wandered up through the Warren, diverting along a lower path that took him onto the rocks below the under cliff, heading towards the *Albemarle*. There were no wreckers in sight.

"Where is everyone?" he asked the lone fishwife he met.

"Well it's Sunday, isn't it — day o' rest," she confided in the slightly insolent local manner.

He knew this was nonsense. He'd seen villagers working

day and night on the wreck for weeks. He trod carefully across the rocks, the sea breaking to his right. He'd learnt how to avoid slipping on the rocks: avoid seaweed, dry surfaces before wet, barnacles and limpets, before smooth, at right-angles to ridged surface. Looking up, he saw the ravine ahead. The *Albemarle* was gone. Washed away by the sea in the night just as the weather had ameliorated.

☽ ☉ ☾

Willcock seemed quite philosophical about the loss.

"Oh dear!"

"Well, that's the end of that then," concluded Beawes.

"Oh, no! that's just the beginning."

"What do you mean?"

"The ship lies on the seabed somewhere, its cargo — most of it — still intact. It is salvageable. It will need to be searched for though. When we find it, divers will need to be employed."

"Divers under the sea? Is that even possible?"

"Absolutely."

"You don't mean Indian pearl divers, do you?"

"No, white men like you and me, in wooden and leather suits, with tubes down which air is pumped to them from boats."

"It seems odd that you know so much despite having lived here... when I've been all over the oceans and..."

"I travel by sea on business to France and Jersey. I sometimes deal with the Port Authorities in Falmouth, Fowey and Plymouth. I read newspapers and books."

"But diving?"

"Have you not read the classics — Herodotus — Alexander the Great was conveyed underwater to see the deeps thousands of years ago."

"Who is going to pay for searchers and divers?"

"The owners, once you release the cargo manifest to them."

"Will they, though?"

"Wouldn't you, if you were an investor and saw a possible

profit of tenfold for an outlay of one?"

"Who is going to supply these searchers and divers?" but Beawes had the answer even before the words were out of his mouth.

☽ ☯ ☾

Willcock discussed the *Albemarle's* diamonds with his wife, something he always did when faced with intractable problems. He had sworn her to secrecy and trusted her word as much as her judgement.

"We can't just take them," he explained.

"Why not? Can I have a peek?"

"If they are not handed in, we will have a regiment of soldiers down here looking for them. That will disrupt our other interests. And no, you can't see them. They are well hidden away for now."

"Couldn't you take a few?"

"No!" As always, talking to his wife, such a beautiful creature, always set one end of his body, or the other, astir. He had an idea.

☽ ☯ ☾

Now the ship had sunk, Beawes expected life in the village to slow down. Instead, he noticed that there was a lot of coming and going at night, along with the dyeing of old sails and tarpaulins. Barrows with spades and picks and crowbars were pushed up the Warren, towards the old wreck site. Hawsers and ropes were being taken off to the east too. Could there be another wreck? Many ships had been wrecked in the storms. He took a walk towards Talland, but there was nothing there. Yet he hadn't overtaken anyone. It was a mystery. He had to accept the only explanation he got, which was that the villagers were working on erecting a new barn in Killigarth. Why would you need old worn sails for that? And why dye them grey?

☽ � ☾

Willcock regarded Beawes benignly.

"I've been considering. I want you to have free choice of several futures. I'd like us all to come out of this safe and happy."

Beawes was unsure what he meant by this unusually trite statement. The hour was late and he wished to retire to bed.

Willcock's knowing eyes seemed to comprehend this and he continued,

"When you go up to your room, you'll find that I have left a surprise for you."

Beawes sighed to himself. There had been several attempts to run him alongside various pretty village maidens. There was one in particular who'd caught his attention. Willcock could arrange anything, but Beawes did not feel ready for any serious involvement. He climbed the stairs steadily. Would he find the pert Nessa warming his bed? It would be rude to refuse. In the dark of his room, he stumbled and fell over a hard, knee-high, object. Scrambling to his feet he laboriously lit an oil lamp. And there sat his sea-chest of private trade from the ship. It was undone. With fumbling fingers, he lifted the lid and held the lamp closer to inspect the contents. It was all there. He felt strangely and immensely grateful — he laughed to himself — at being given his own property back. In this place, it seemed an outstandingly generous act. His relief and happiness from this act of friendship, as much as anything else, overwhelmed him and tears came to his eyes.

When he had recovered, he bounced downstairs where the Willcocks were pretending to do other things: Mrs Willcock knitting, Thomas Willcock reading a book; but both grinning. Many questions arose in Beawes's head but he didn't care, he just embraced both of them in turn. He had no words.

"So now, if you want to give up the sea, you can open an inn or buy a farm, if that's what you want. Or sail my privateer once it is built."

"Yes."

"And it doesn't matter what the Court of the East India Company decides about the *Albemarle*."

"Thank you. But how?"

"Personally, I never question good fortune."

"Won't it look a little odd that I made it off the ship with my own private trade?"

"You worry too much. Now to bed, all of us, there is a lot to do in the morning."

The gentle corruption of Captain Thomas Beawes was complete.

☽ ☯ ☾

"Show us what you bought in the East Indies."

Beawes was delighted to do so, laying out each package like a rich man's child at Christmas, explaining as he unwrapped each one.

"This is jade. You can tell it's the real thing as it feels waxy and cold to the tongue."

Willcock nodded and admired each piece. Beawes continued,

"This package has the finest silks." Unrestrained, he undid the tape around the small bundle and the shiny silks erupted from their confinement in a burst of bright colours — reds, yellows, greens, blue and purples.

Willcock had rarely seen him so buoyant.

"And this has pearls of quite good quality and size." He poured the glistening roundels across the silks.

"These are valuable spices of all kinds: saffron, cloves, nutmeg…"

Willcock knew how to be patient, and was genuinely enjoying his friend's pleasure.

Mrs Willcock peered from a distance and said nothing.

Beawes noticed her and waved his hand across his hoard.

"Please choose something for yourself — as a keepsake."

"That's very kind. Perhaps tomorrow, some little thing."

Willcock scratched his right eyebrow with his left hand and

Mrs Willcock said her "Goodnights" and left.

There were only a few packages left. Some contained tea and coffee. The last three packages were enclosed within leather wallets.

Proudly Beawes disclosed his treasure.

"My main investment: diamonds, rubies and emeralds."

Willcock counted 40 diamonds, 20 rubies and 20 emeralds; of differing sizes. Some were quite large, most were uncut, and some very simply cut.

"Do you know what they are worth, and the quality?"

"I asked the supercargo, Bullock, to come along with me when I bought them. They are not wonderful quality, just what I could afford."

"What will you do with them? How will you turn them into money and at what profit?"

"Well, they'll have to be sold in London, perhaps auctioned. Bullock reckoned I'd at least quadruple my investment on the stones."

"How much did you spend on them? If you don't mind confiding in me."

"Four hundred pounds, most of my life's savings."

"I have to buy goods in Jersey. Small, highly valuable stones like these would be more useful than having to carry gold."

Beawes said nothing and waited.

"Will you consider selling the stones to me for one thousand, eight hundred pounds?"

"When?"

"Now. You'll get a fair price and a gold coin immediately, and you wouldn't have to pay commission to anyone."

Beawes considered the matter. There couldn't be anything sinister in this offer. He felt guilty immediately for even thinking so. Willcock could have taken all of it, and he would have been none the wiser, thinking it lost in the sunken *Albemarle*. Now there was a thought.

"How did you save my box of wealth?"

"It was luck. You told me where it was in the ship, so I made a special trip to get it before anyone else did, or the ship sunk. It turns out that I was just in time. I wouldn't tell anyone — you know jealousy, and the people in London might think it strange."

"Thank you, once again I'm most grateful."

"Think about my offer for the stones — there is some leeway on it. I understand if you want to take them to London and try for a better price."

"No. I've thought about it — I accept."

Willcock offered his hand and Beawes shook it warmly.

Willcock looked him in the eye, "You've done the right thing, Thomas. If you had taken them to London, you'd find there were a lot of other diamonds and precious stones on the market by then — especially once the *Albemarle's* ones hit the market."

"The *Albemarle's*? but it sunk."

"Ah! I thought it would be best to keep that secret until now. I found the diamonds and took them off the ship as soon as I heard about them. They are in safe-keeping. Tomorrow, I will send a letter, which I would like you and the supercargoes to sign, telling London that the diamonds have been saved. I intend to inform London that they'll be despatched securely as soon as it can be arranged with Plymouth."

"Why didn't you tell me? This will change everything... the attitude of the Company, I mean. They'll be so pleased with this recovery that they'll likely overlook the minor infringements of rules. Knowing the diamonds are safe, they'll probably be content with losing the ship, and the rest of its cargo."

"Good, so that's all settled then. Perhaps we could mention in the letter that I was the one who found the diamonds and handed them over — I'll need a receipt, of course."

☽ ☯ ☾

The following morning, Mrs Willcock chose a green jade gem, carved in the shape of a dolphin, which she hoped to turn into a brooch. "The same colour as your eyes, my love," Mr Willcock observed.

Beawes and Bullock, the Chief Supercargo, quickly checked

the bulses of precious stones against the cargo manifest, counting the diamonds, rubies and emeralds in each pocket and carefully retying the laces of the leather pockets again. Addis and Ustick repeated the task before signing a receipt, which Willcock ensured, was witnessed by the *Albemarle's* first lieutenant and the attorney from Bodmin.

🌒 🌕 🌘

The Company were delighted at the news of the diamond recovery. Talk was now of "good Captain Beawes" instead of "that fool Beawes", which was unfortunate because they had just sent him a letter of admonishment for not responding to their previous correspondence summoning him to London. The letter, when it arrived, puzzled him as he'd not received the previous letters.

There followed the formalities of handing the diamonds over from one official to another, involving a trail of receipts along the way, and guarded conveyance from Polperro to Looe, to Plymouth to Portsmouth and on to the East India House in London.

🌒 🌕 🌘

The law was being thwarted. At any house in Polperro, a guest would be offered fine tobacco and coffee, the likes of which would grace a London gentleman's club. Meals were served on fine blue and white Chinese porcelain. Locals vied with one another to create recipes using the exotic spices until the alleys and streets smelt of the Orient. So much stolen cargo in such a relatively small population resulted in a glut, and pounds of coffee were exchanged for a few pence. Meanwhile, relieved at the recovery of the diamonds, the Company decided to take a pragmatic view of the situation in far-away Cornwall. What had been officially salvaged or retrieved from the ship's cargo was dried out and renovated where possible, then sold off cheaply in Plymouth. They gave up trying to prosecute the locals, locally. They gave up trying to change the laws, so offenders could be tried in London. In the end, business acumen overtook outrage and, swallowing their considerable pride, they offered to buy back the coffee, tea, pepper, spices and textiles at rock bottom prices, no questions were asked.

They did, however, sign a one-year contract with a local fisherman to search for the sunken *Albemarle* using the old methods of glass-bottomed buckets and local knowledge of tidal flows. If it was found, then the employment of a diver would be the next step. That unusually civilised and literate local, Mr Thomas Willcock, had it all in hand. His invoices for reimbursement for accommodation, food and drink for the crew, and other sundries, arrived at East India House at the height of the diamond euphoria. Comptroller Wooley signed them off for payment with, almost, a flourish.

☽ ☯ ☾

Someone informed against Willcock, stating he'd been involved in looting the *Albemarle*. The Vicar of Llansallos was suspected to be the informer and was branded a bad sport, and an even worse Cornishman. Sour grapes was thought to be behind it. Shortly afterwards, Bishop Trelawney, having heard of Cumming's raid on the *Albemarle* and the court summons, intervened so that, by arrangement, the offending cleric was forced to pay £20 in compensation. A worse punishment was his mandatory journey to see the Bishop, where he received the most prolonged and frightening reprimand — of biblical ferocity — of his life.

Willcock, in light of testimonials from Captain Beawes and his crew: as their rescuer and host, his role in saving the diamonds, protecting the ship from raids by the tinners and Vicar James Cumming, was exonerated. The accusation was considered vindictive and the prosecuting lawyer in Bodmin was ordered to drop the case by the mighty Court of the East India Company. And, of course, Willcock was still useful.

Bridging a tiny cove under the cliffs, and unseen from the coastal path, was a curious structure only visible from very close or from within. Often, it was shrouded in mist. Occasionally, the sun shone through gaps in the shrouds and worn sails that covered it, permeating into the gloom where men worked day and night. Rocks and boulders were stacked all around the mastless hull, the bowsprit had been removed. To any accessible eyes, it was nothing more than a piece of rocky coastline that was no different from its surroundings. Every night, goods from the hold would be moved to hiding places in and around Polperro. Some particular items, intrinsic to the *Albemarle*, were put aside for a special purpose. Once the holds were empty and if the hulk could not be moved and sunk, it would end as an overnight blaze. The sea and sands of the coast would do the rest.

The bulses arrived at the Controller's desk in April. He regarded the five leather bundles, which, when undone, unrolled into a long strip with tied pockets containing the precious stones. The Controller was satisfied that each pocket was labelled with the count of each stone type, its description and carat weight, all of which were expected to agree with the cargo manifest. Weeks later, the Company diamond experts, a Jew and a Dutchman, who were on a retainer, became available. They settled at a nearby long table and set-up their equipment, loupes and optical devices, prisms, the latest microscopes, tweezers, fine weights and arrays of tiny blades and touchstones. They began their comparison of each stone and its manifest entry, a task that had them labouring for many weeks. Their final report highlighted considerable discrepancy between the descriptions of some of the stones and the manifest. A significant proportion were not as described, and were of much reduced quality and value. Somewhere between the Indies, South America, Cornwall and the passage to London, they had been switched.

☽ ☯ ☾

In July of 1709, the fishing vessel started fulfilling its contract, searching for the sunken wreck of the *Albemarle*. It sailed back and forth, its four crew diligently leaning over the side with their long glass-bottomed buckets, wearing dark hoods to enhance their view of the seabed. Some cannons were lifted and the owners paid a third of the value for the salvers.

In August of 1709, Willcock, Captain Beawes and his officers, the supercargoes, and all the officials at Plymouth and Portsmouth — wherever they were — received letters. Inside were orders for them to report to a lawyer and swear an enclosed affidavit confirming that they had no knowledge of the whereabouts of any lost or stolen diamonds or precious stones from the *Albemarle*, and that they were not in possession of any of them. They were all very puzzled, except for Willcock. Even Beawes was confused, at least for a few days.

In response to the stick of increasingly stern letters and the carrot of a new command, Beawes visited East India House in London in the autumn of 1709. Despite his reluctance to attend, especially given his new and secret alternative future choices of career, he knew he needed to play the dutiful Captain. It was easy enough to profess ignorance about the fate of the diamonds. He referred them to his affidavit. His sparse communication with London was less easily explained though. They offered him a new ship but refused to let him choose his officers, which suggested a lack of trust. Having possible "spies" thrust upon him and the loss of patronage to select officers from the *Albemarle* did not appeal. So he refused. He put in a claim for compensation for his lost private trade — a dishonesty that he admitted to himself with little trouble from his conscience. They reduced his request for twenty-five percent of what had been recovered to five percent. They even fined him £20 for breaching orders. The directors received Beawes's polite thanks for their munificence, with no sense of irony. In the face of such meanness, he saw no reason to satisfy their curiosity about his plans for the future.

In the spring of 1710, not long before their contract expired, the fishermen searchers hauled the ship's bell of the *Albemarle* into their fishing boat, along with some sodden bundles of cargo and, amazingly, the ship's figurehead, which had been expected to have floated away. With such substantial evidence, who could doubt that this was the final resting place of the ship? It was explained that the putative wreck site was spread over a fairly wide area and, although quite shallow, was on the edge of an underwater cliff. The sea could sweep the remnants into the depths of the cliffs with the onset of any fierce storm. The searchers were paid off.

Amazingly, the East India Company then signed a contract for a diver, working for Thomas Willcock, to search the apparent location of the wreck. It seems as though they were convinced that the remaining cargo, as long as it had not been broached, would be suitable for drying out and renovation. Some waterlogged cargo was recovered and treated. The diver was paid off.

"Captain Smith", who had a South Welsh accent, put his new command, the privateer *Audacity* and its crew, through its paces, finishing with a six-gun salute for his patrons, the Willcocks. Thomas Willcock shook his head and waved his little expenses notebook in mock disapproval at the expense of gunpowder. Mrs Willcock, wearing a green jade brooch and a rather fine diamond ring slapped him playfully on the arm.

Eventually, the pen pushers at East India Company brought the case to the attention of the Controller, Mr Wooley, and he read the whole sad history. Then, stacking suspicion upon suspicion, paid all outstanding charges, muttered "Barbarians" and closed the file.

Historical Note

The facts regarding the wreck of the *Albemarle* can be found in the late James Derriman's excellent book "The Wreck of the *Albemarle*", in the records of The British Library and the archives of Looe Museum.

The outstanding mysteries that remain of this shipwreck are: the *Albemarle's* final resting place, and what happened to the diamonds?

In that terrible month of December 1708, the *Albemarle* was wrecked near Polperro. Then, after a few weeks, it disappeared, having apparently washed-off and sunk elsewhere.

The fate of the diamonds was uncertain at first. A reward of 1,000 guineas and the offer of a government pardon was published in the London Gazette in December, 1709. The next we heard of them was in a letter stating that they have been recovered. Although, six months later, various people, who would have had some involvement with the diamonds, were asked to sign affidavits stating that they have not taken any of the precious stones, were not aware of anyone else who had, and did not claim any reward. Why?

I have speculated rationally about the diamonds, and perhaps more wildly about the final fate of the ship. Many ships were wrecked during that stormy month of December in 1708. There were reports of other vessels meeting disaster on the Rannies at the back of Looe Island.

The location of "Lazy Cove" is also a mystery. I have made a guess at how the name of this place might have arisen by word of mouth, but not on any map. Some decades after the wreck, the name occurs again when it is used to give the location of a small leisure building — "at Lazy Cove" — East of Polperro. I think that I may have found at least the site of this small building.

Little is known about the real Thomas Willcock or Captain Beawes, so again I have used my imagination concerning their character profiles, based on their behaviour towards the authorities and vice versa.

I do not know whether anyone died during the shipwreck — apart from two monkeys — but, with so many letters and documents missing from the records, I felt free to expand the story as I thought fit.

Polperro Harbour

Model of *The George of Looe* (shown by kind permission of
East Looe Town Trust)

The Lost Bell of the *George* of Looe.

1588 & now?

In the Guildhall of East Looe, there are a set of stained glass windows that celebrate the history of Looe. In themselves, they are of no great age, having been made in late Victorian times. Yet they are a cornucopia of folk memory. One of the windows depicts a ship — the *George* of Looe — sailing forth to fight the Spanish Armada in 1588. In the Looe Museum, there is a wonderful model of the *George* of Looe, made by the late Bernie Doyle. So why has the name of this Looe-built craft lived on?

Little is known about the *George* of Looe itself, other than the fact that several ships of that name were built over the years. The subsequent ones were named in honour of the first, that was famed for its battle against several enemy ships in some unknown combat. All are ships of lost renown. Later, when the Royal Navy was formed, the name lived on in a series of ships named H.M.S. *George*.

If that armed merchantman, together with many other ships, had not set sail and harried the Armada to its doom, perhaps history would have been different. The reformation might have been overturned and the Mayflower might not have left Plymouth for the Americas, thirty-two years later.

Following years of suspicion and antagonism between Catholic Spain and Protestant England, the execution of Mary, Queen of Scots, angered Philip of Spain. It was enough for him to, perhaps prematurely, launch his great Enterprise of England.

The Spanish Armada of 1588 sailed from Lisbon in May and reached southwest England on July 30th. The Spanish planned to pass along the Channel and guard the army of the Duke of Parma as it was ferried across from the Spanish Netherlands to invade England. However, the second-in-command was keen to land somewhere, like the Isle of Wight, if practicable.

Warning beacons blazed all along the south coast and church bells rang in warning. Soldiers and cannons were spread thinly across vulnerable places to combat any landing attempts.

The huge Spanish ships carried many soldiers who hoped to board and overwhelm the smaller English ships. The English ships were more manoeuvrable and their commanders hoped to stand-off and use their greater rate of cannon fire.

The English plan was to harry — and indeed hurry — the Armada up the Channel and away from any potential landing opportunities. For this, the English fleet needed to get to windward of the Spanish fleet. Drake and the English fleet were unable to leave Plymouth until the tide changed. It is possible that messages were sent to ports to the westward to get ships out behind the Spanish as they passed by. This would keep Spanish eyes on the English ships to their landward side, whilst the main English fleet sailed across in front, well out of sight, and around the southern side of the Spanish, with the intention of suddenly appearing behind them.

The *George* of Looe would have been one of the ships that sallied forth as the Armada as it passed the Eddystone. One can imagine the ship's bell ringing out, echoing along the harbour as it cast off and made its way out of the haven. Built in Looe, probably along West Looe river, it was a three-masted ocean going merchantman — a bark — carrying 26 iron guns and two brass guns, and a complement of 40 men. Their task would have been to engage and distract, allowing the English fleet to leave Plymouth undetected. The fate of the Armada is well-known. The *George* of Looe then disappears from history, perhaps back to commercial and piratical enterprises.

But what of the ship's bell? Could it have survived over four hundred years?

It all starts in a queue for a bazaar at the Riverside Church, in about 2006. We were waiting for the event to open and for the vicar to bless the proceedings. Small change was being sorted from purses and wallets to obtain suitable entrance donations. I started to chat to the lady behind me — very un-English behaviour — but something we succumb to when happy, and with plenty of time available. Somehow, we started to talk about the local history. I had helped the, then, Museum curator, Barbara Birchwood-Harper, with her work in small ways. I was always gathering snippets of interest.

Lily Williams was the gracious lady in the queue and we became friends over the years, often having coffee together. She is a great conversationalist, who has lived a very interesting life — but that is another story. Lily was very striking in her younger days and photographs of her at that time remind one of Ingrid Bergman.

What is pertinent to our story is that Lily, on a train from London to Cornwall, around 1977, had another chance meeting, this time with Luis Marden, a pioneer underwater photographer employed by National Geographic Magazine.

Recently, I asked Lily to record the part of her story that was relevant to the "George", on tape. It seems appropriate to now revert to a transcript of that tape (edited for the "ums" and "ers" and repetitions that we all intersperse our conversations with — "you know?").

This is the transcript of a recording of Carrick White talking to Lily Williams on 8th December 2015:

How did you meet Luis?

I met him on the train coming down to Cornwall from London. And we got chatting, of course. We exchanged telephone numbers. And then he rang me from Washington on many occasions. And then he mentioned on the way down from London, when I told him I lived in Looe in Cornwall, he asked me if I knew anything about the George *of Looe. Now, I hadn't been in Looe very long and didn't know all the historical facts, but I told him there was a St George's Island just off of Looe and we chatted about that. And he told me that he had, in the past, discovered the bell from a ship called the* George *of Looe and he had brought it up from the coast of the South America somewhere and he had this bell in his 'backyard' amongst many other artefacts.*

Do you know what year that was, roughly…?

It would be about 1977 I think, when my divorce came through. And so we kept in touch and he told me he was going down to Penryn, where he was having a new boat built and to name it Bounty the Second, *which he did. But, unfortunately, it foundered off South America on some uncharted reef. So he lost that boat but he kept in touch with me for a number of years.*

Was he on the boat when it foundered?

Yes, yes, he was taking it back over there, that was on his journey from Cornwall to America.

Just jumping back a bit, when you met him on the train, I suppose the ice was broken because you said you told a couple of kids off?

Yes, it was very good (laughing). These boys came into the compartment — there was nobody else but Luis and I there. They came in and immediately switched on their transistor radio. So, eventually I spoke to them. I said, "Now then boys, I wondered, did you pay for a First Class compartment as the gentleman opposite did? And I require peace and quiet. So if you'll turn your radio off." So they said, "Oh, no, we didn't pay first class" — they just came in. So we chatted a little while. They said we are going to Torquay, "We are hoping to find work there, we've come from

Liverpool." So I said, "Well, I wish you all the luck."

And so we chatted for a while and we ended up with these boys offering [to share] their lunch too [with us]. Ever so nice. But they did go further down the train. They were very decent.

But then he [Luis Marden] writes in one of his letters of how he recalls my encounter with the boys on the train and my admonishment of them. I think he was just amused by it all because it ended with the offer to share their lunch.

Was he quite well dressed?

Oh, yes, I really thought he was some sort of MP or a businessman. He was so immaculate.

And he used to go to Cornwall when he came over here sometimes?

Oh, yes.

The Pandora was mentioned…?

The Pandora Inn down at Restronguet, near Falmouth. He later telephoned me from Washington to ask me if I wished to accompany him to the Pandora as he was in possession of a spike from the Bounty that he had brought up with many others, and that he wanted to present one to the Pandora Inn that had been bought by the Captain [Edwards] of the Pandora [who] had bought the inn with the money he was paid by the Government for bringing back the mutineers. And so, in the Pandora Inn they had a very large replica of the Pandora in a glass case. So Luis presented this spike to the landlord, but the landlord, I thought, was not very interested.

Oh, dear …

And, so, anyway I read that replica [sic] had been sold by auction somewhere. I think in Plymouth. And I was disappointed as I would have loved to have bought it.

Yes, yes.

So we kept in touch for many years. I was very sad to learn that he had died, but he was at least ninety.

He couldn't have had a more exciting life could he?

No! he could not! He was a close friend of the King and Queen Salote of Tonga. I have the postcard in my possession he sent me, saying I am at the wedding of the King of Nepal. He had taught King Hussein of Jordan to dive. At one time... when I went down to the Pandora and met him, he said I've only got four days as I've just been given a visa to go into China — he was studying bamboos of the world.

Did he ever meet Cousteau?

Oh yes he was a close friend of Jacques Cousteau, and he used to go with him on the...

The *Calypso*.

Yes... So he was a very close friend.

Did he know Richard Larne, the shipwreck guy over here?

I've never heard of him. But we had a meal at the Lobster Pot Inn, Mousehole. I thought it was very amusing as there were some divers at the next table and very loudly showing-off about their diving and there was Luis sitting next to them. He didn't say a word. He was a very respectable and decent man and I felt very safe and comfortable with him.

Yes.

It's been very interesting and if I can help you in any other way ...

No, that's fine. It's given me a lot of information — thank you.

You're very welcome. It'll give you a good interest.

Indeed.

(Tape off. Tape on)
Could you just say that again?

It would give me the greatest pleasure to have that bell returned to Looe, to the place where it ought to be. I am 88 years old. Whether I will live long enough to see this happen I don't know, but I'm sure that you will do your best, and thank you.

End of transcript.

Incidentally, Lily is 88 years old now and largely housebound. Yet her memory is excellent, as evidenced by information she gave me concerning a local underground passage, with entrances from a well and a trapdoor in the dining-room, for a certain old house (which, for reasons of confidentiality, I am not disclosing).

"In my backyard" was the intriguing remark made by Luis Marden about the whereabouts of the ship's bell of the *George* of Looe. Where was his "backyard"? Since 1959, and until he went into a home suffering from Parkinson's disease, roughly in 1998, Luis lived at The Marden House, Maclean, Virginia, USA. He died in 2003. His wife lived on at their property before going into a retirement home.

In the late 1950s, Luis and his wife had been fishing in the rapids of the River Potomac when, enthralled by the beautiful surroundings, he espied a ledge on a nearby cliff. It was, he realised, a unique site for a house and he bought the land. He engaged the eminent architect, Frank Lloyd Wright, to design a house to fit the plot, and also design and commission bespoke furniture for it.

This was one of Wright's last designs. The house was long and fairly narrow, rather like a boat, with views out through a huge picture window onto the rapids far below. The garden or yard was also long and narrow and Luis insisted on it being terraced to provide a downward aspect to the river.

It was ironic that Frank Lloyd Wright was a minimalist and hated clutter whereas Luis filled the house with artefacts and mementoes collected in his travels all over the world.

Following the deaths of the Mardens, a wealthy businessman, Jim Kimsey, who owned a large adjoining property, bought The Marden House, which had become somewhat run down. Due to a misunderstanding with one of his employees, a sale of the furniture began. This caused an uproar from various Frank Lloyd Wright societies, and Mr Kimsey kindly bought the furniture back and renovated the house. This was done at the expense of one million dollars. Subsequently, Mr Kimsey, always a fan of Ethel Marden, became a fan of Frank Lloyd Wright, too. He retains the property for small private dinner parties, where he is confident that his guests will be astonished by the wonderful view.

If the bell is anywhere, it is in that garden — Luis's backyard.

The bell was probably made of bronze, therefore not worth much — a few thousand pounds or dollars perhaps? If it is there, it will likely be covered in earth and undergrowth.

It will certainly give a loud, non-ferrous signal to a metal detector though.

If it's not there, then perhaps it fell over the edge of the cliff, or it might have been "liberated" for use as a bell on a house or boat.

There is always a possibility that Luis may have made the story up to impress a lady, but that seems very unlikely based on how the conversation went. Having lived such a fabulous life himself, there was no need to boast or fabricate. This was a man who was intimate with Kings and Queens and Princes. He was friends with the legendary Jacques Cousteau. He was friends with King Hussein of Jordan. He had discovered the wreck of *HMS Bounty*. He had an orchid named after him. He had been granted one of the first visas to visit China after the revolution, to carry out research on bamboos.

On balance, I believe that it is still there in Luis's "backyard", with the Potomac rapids roaring away below.

There have been three attempts to get someone — Mr Kimsey, US newspapers, the National Geographic — to search for the bell. Of course, this doesn't necessarily mean that Mr Kimsey actually ever saw the letters.

But who in the States has ever heard of a little fishing town called Looe, in Cornwall?

I suspect that all correspondence went straight into the waste paper bin or shredder.

In my last attempt (the fourth), I wrote to Mr Kimsey, enclosing a book about the history of Looe as a gift and this story, but the package was returned — "Not known at this address".

Would it be possible to try one more time? It would require the backing of the Looe Town Council, our local MP, and an approach to the US Ambassador.

What a wonder, what a re-affirmation of — I won't say Special Relationship — but friendship, between the Old World and the New; Britain and the USA; Cornwall and Virginia, if the bell of the *George* of Looe (or even a photograph of it) could be presented to the people and town of Looe.

The George of Looe in a stained glass window of
Guildhall (shown by kind permission of East Looe
Town Trust)

Non-historical notes!

So how much is fact and how much is fiction?

Hartman's Luck: I could not find out why Hartman was ordered back from India. I am unsure whether he'd upset the Indian nobility, or the Danish authorities at home, or both. I also do not know if he was planning to build a fort there. Whether he ever actually met George Reynolds, who soon after became a pirate, or was in collusion with him, I am unclear about. All of the rest is substantially true.

Murder at Morval: I invented the treachery of Lord Glyn's deputy. Based on the timings of how far Glyn's party would have travelled, given the approximate times stated in the records, for the departure from Morval and the attack, I worked out and discovered the putative ambush site. I speculated his reasons for going to Tavistock, given his vulnerable situation. All of the rest is true.

The Battle of Braddock Down: I have (reasonably) supposed that the Parliamentarian army was led astray by secretly hostile local scouts. As such, I have, perhaps outrageously, suggested a concealed, but confined, advance through the high-banked hollow lanes towards Boconnoc, as a surprise attack. The rest is true.

The **Albemarle,** ***by the Grace of God, ours!:*** The early part of Willcock's life, before he arrived at Polperro, is a figment of my imagination. I do not know what became of Captain Beawes a year or so after the shipwreck, and beyond. The audacity of the Polperro people and the "spiv" like cunning of Willcock was amazing. Therefore, I have been just as outrageous in extending their exploits, by suggesting that the ship did not simply wash off of the rocks and sink somewhere unknown, but was deliberately moved for a short while so that they could continue looting it before destroying it. After all, the Royal Navy were considering re-floating it. Again, I have imagined an explanation for the "first you see them, now you don't" nature of the diamonds' recovery, the apparent "non-recovery", and the demand for affidavits, as recorded in the records of the East India Company. The rest is true.

The Lost Bell of the George of Looe: all true, except that there may have been several ships named George of Looe, perhaps going back from Elizabethan times to Henry VIII, or even earlier medieval times. We cannot be sure which ship Luis Marden's bell came from, but it is unlikely to be earlier as Columbus did not discover the Americas until 1492. It was only in the Elizabethan era that ships would sail as far afield as South America.

Peter and Pedro: The first place Pedro (or Pero) el Nino attacked was Shitta or Chita; this was the name of "Looe" at the time, as evidenced by Shutta Lane. The more affluent lived tucked away from the sea. The river bends at the estuary, and the harbour was further concealed from the sea by rocks at the entrance, which were removed in Victorian times. Purposefully, little was visible at the estuary in order to avoid attracting marauders from the open sea. For the same reason, in the harbour, buildings were built low down by the water, or along lateral creeks and quays. These would be small settlements with local names. I believe the description in the records fits Looe/Chita better than anywhere else (see *Defending the Island*, by Norman Longmate, p303-5). However, I'm uncertain about the deployment of the galleys once within the river. There were no harbour walls, just beaches, so mooring their galleys to the bridge is almost certain. I have imagined the attack on the small hamlet of Portbodriggan (now West Looe) nearer the estuary. They would have been foolish not to have secured such a place that was behind them, and from which there could have been an attempt to block the river or prevent their withdrawal in some other way.

CW